# THE
# UNDISCOVERED
# CHEKHOV

# THE UNDISCOVERED CHEKHOV

## Thirty-Eight New Stories

## Anton Chekhov

Translated by
PETER CONSTANTINE

SEVEN STORIES PRESS
NEW YORK • TORONTO • LONDON

*In the U.K.:*
Turnaround Publisher Services Ltd., Unit 3, Olympia Trading Estate, Coburg Road, Wood Green, London N22 6TZ U.K.

*In Canada:*
Hushion House, 36 Northline Road, Toronto, Ontario M4B 3E2, Canada

Library of Congress Cataloging-in-Publication Data

Chekhov, Anton Pavlovich, 1860–1904.
[Short stories. English. Selections]
The undiscovered Chekhov: thirty-eight new stories / by Anton Chekhov; translated by Peter Constantine. —Seven Stories Press 1st ed.
p.    cm.
ISBN 1-888363-76-2
1. Chekhov, Anton Pavlovich, 1860–1904—Translations into English.
I. Constantine, Peter, 1963–    . II. Title.
PG3456.A15C66 1998
891.73'3—dc21                                   98–34461
CIP

9 8 7 6 5 4 3 2 1

Book design by Martin Moskof

Seven Stories Press
140 Watts Street
New York, NY 10013

Printed in the U.S.A.

# CONTENTS

# INTRODUCTION

"**W**RITE AS MUCH AS you can!! Write, write, write till your fingers break!" This advice, which Anton Chekhov sent to Maria Kiselyova in a letter in 1886, was the motto by which he lived and worked. He was twenty-six, and had already published over four hundred short stories and vignettes in popular magazines, as well as two books of stories, with a third in the making. He had written his first series of plays, *Fatherlessness, Diamond Cut Diamond, The Scythe Struck the Stone, Why the Hen Cackled, The Clean-shaven Secretary with the Pistol,* and *The Nobleman* (none of which have come down to us), and *Platonov* and *On the High Road,* and he was about to begin writing *Ivanov,* his first major theatrical success.

Throughout this period Chekhov was also energetically studying medicine at Moscow University, from which he graduated in June 1884. The nameplate on the Chekhov family's door now read "Dr. A. P. Chekhov."

The stories and vignettes in *The Undiscovered Chekhov* are from this period, the most prolific of Chekhov's life. They are some of the works that helped make him a literary star and contributed to his receiving the Pushkin Prize in 1888. None of these works has appeared in any English-language Chekhov collection, and all but two have never before been translated into English. ("To Speak or Be Silent: A Tale" appeared in the *Nation* in 1954, and "The Good German" in the *Quarterly Review of Literature* in 1962.)

For Chekhov, these early years were extremely difficult. The Russian literary giants of the nineteenth century—Tolstoy, Pushkin, Gogol, Turgenev, and Dostoevsky—had all come from the nobility. Chekhov was the grandson of a serf. His father had run a ramshackle grocery store in Taganrog, in southern Russia. When Chekhov was sixteen, his father went bankrupt and left town in a hurry. He took the whole family, including the two elder sons, with him to Moscow—everyone, that is, except for young Anton, who was left destitute and penniless to fend for himself in Taganrog.

As Chekhov wrote to his friend and publisher Suvorin many years later, "What the aristocrat writers get for free from nature, intellectuals of lower birth have to pay for with their youth. Write a story of how a young man, the son of a serf, a former shopboy, choirboy, schoolboy, and student, brought up to respect rank, to kiss priests' hands, and worship the thoughts of others, thankful for every piece of bread, whipped time and again, having to go give lessons without galoshes, brawling, torturing animals, loving to eat at rich relatives' houses, needlessly hypocritical before God and man, merely from a sense of his own insignificance—write a story about how this young man squeezes the serf out of himself, drop by drop, and how waking up one bright morning this young man feels that in his veins there no longer flows the blood of a slave, but the blood of a real man."

By the time the nineteen-year-old Chekhov rejoined his parents in Moscow three years later, having secured a scholarship to study at the university, the family was living in utter poverty in grimy basement lodgings in Grachyovka, one of Moscow's red-light districts. Anton immediately took charge and became the head and chief support of the family, a position he was to keep till the end of his life. His family nicknamed him "Papa Antosha." He was determined to succeed, and despite the harsh reality of his situation wrote to his cousin, "I will make a fortune... that is as certain as that two and two make four."

Chekhov began making his fortune by writing stories and vignettes for the popular Moscow and St. Petersburg magazines. According to his younger brother Michael, the moment

---

the first installment of Anton's scholarship arrived from Taganrog, he bought up all the magazines he could lay his hands on. He meticulously read through them to see what they were publishing, and then went to work. He sent in sharp, witty, innovative pieces such as "On the Train," "Sarah Bernhardt Comes to Town," and "The Trial," all of which were published during 1881 in the Moscow humorous magazine *Zritel* (Spectator). "Confession—or Olya, Zhenya, Zoya: A Letter" was published in *Budilnik* (Alarm Clock), and "Village Doctors" in *Svet i teni* (Light and Shades).

Chekhov's pieces came as a surprise to readers of the time, for whom a story was supposed to deal with significant issues and have a clear beginning, middle, and end. It was supposed to impart the author's ideals. Chekhov's stories veered from this norm. "On the Train" is seemingly formless and impressionistic: the protagonist travels through the night on a train that then breaks down. Nothing actually happens, except that he meets a series of bizarre figures: a pickpocket, a lost peasant, a man wishing he had some chloroform so he can have his way with the girl sitting next to him. The atmosphere is oppressive—"Darkness, anguish, thoughts of death, memories of childhood, oh God!"—but Chekhov constantly weaves in bright flashes of humor and comedy that give the piece its complex texture. In "Sarah Bernhardt Comes to Town" Chekhov is even more innovative and daring. The story is

---

narrated as a string of disjointed telegrams. In this period Chekhov signed his pieces "Antosha," "Antosha Ch.," "My brother's brother," "A man without a spleen," and "Chekhonte"—the last a nickname coined for him by his former religion teacher at school, Father Pokrovsky.

Contemporaries of Chekhov described him roaming the streets, markets, taverns, and brothels of Moscow, absorbing the color and commotion of the city and working it into quick, vivid prose. His friend and fellow writer Vladimir Korolenko wrote in his memoirs that when he asked Chekhov how he wrote his stories, Chekhov laughed, snatched up the nearest object—an ashtray—and said that if Korolenko wanted a story called "The Ashtray," he could have it the next morning.

Soon Chekhov was writing at such a pace that he was paying family and friends 10 kopecks for story ideas and 20 kopecks for plot outlines. But making ends meet remained a major problem for him throughout the 1880s, and in letters to friends he constantly laments his lack of money. In a letter to Suvorin in 1888 Chekhov wrote, "I was terribly corrupted by the fact that I was born, grew up, studied, and began to write in a milieu in which money played a shockingly large role."

As money began trickling in from the publication of his work, Chekhov managed to move his family to better lodgings—they were to move almost a dozen times during his student years. But as he had to share his cramped living space with his parents, siblings, lodgers, and a constant flow of visiting relatives, Chekhov's living and working conditions remained very difficult.

"In front of me sits my nonliterary work, banging mercilessly at my conscience. In the next room a visiting relative's fledgling is bawling; in the other room father is reading The Sealed Angel out loud to mother. Someone has wound up the phonograph, and La Belle Hélène is playing. I want to escape to the country, but it's one in the morning. Can you imagine more vile circumstances for a man of letters?"

Chekhov wrote this to his new friend and publisher Nicholas Leikin in August 1883. Leikin was the owner and editor of the popular humorous St. Petersburg magazine *Oskolki* (Splinters), for which Chekhov was to write 162 pieces over the next couple of years. Leikin had been searching for an energetic writer who had a wild sense of humor and an innovative style—and, most importantly, who was a master of brevity. Chekhov was the ideal candidate. *Oskolki* had a strict editorial limit of 100 lines, which forced Chekhov to develop an inventive style concise enough to carry ideas within an extremely restrictive framework. He complained bitterly that he had to "squeeze the very pith and essence" out of his plots, but he readily complied, sending Leikin some of the most original writing of the time. *Oskolki* published everything from anecdotes, witty riddles, and cartoons to intricate vignettes and stories. Chekhov took these forms and expanded them into new literary genres. In one of the first pieces *Oskolki* published, "An Unsuccessful Visit," a simple joke turns into what today would be classified as a short short story. It begins, "A dandy enters a house in which he's never been." There is a swift roll of dialogue in which the debonair young man's roguish language bounces off the sensitive, nuanced responses of a young girl "wearing a cotton dress and little white apron." The delicate vignette ends with a one-liner that turns it right back into a comic anecdote.

In another early piece published in *Oskolki,* "The Cross," Chekhov pokes a daring jab at the oppressive state censorship, which had just been granted greater power after the assassination of Czar Alexander II in March 1881. In "The Cross," a poet enters a drawing room: "'Well,' the hostess turns to him, 'how did your dear little poem do?'" The guests hover about him, amazed and impressed that a poet should be awarded a cross for a poem. The angry poet holds up his manuscript for all to see, and the startled guests realize that the cross he was awarded is "not the kind of cross you can pin on your lapel"—it is the red ink cross of the state censor. His poem has been disallowed.

Like many of his contemporaries, Chekhov put a good deal of effort into eluding the censor. It was always chancy what would manage to slip by and what would be prohibited. The story "In Autumn," for instance, passed the censor and was published in *Budilnik* in 1882. But three years later, when Chekhov adapted it as the one-act play *On the High Road*, a drama censor with the eye-catching name of Kaiser von Nilckheim branded it filthy and foul. It was not performed during Chekhov's lifetime. The short story "To Speak or Be Silent" was also forbidden by the censor, as it warned the reader of the dangers of speaking too freely before a stranger who might well be a secret service agent.

In "Intrigues," Chekhov anticipates modernism. He builds up, element by element, a psychological portrait of an eccentric physician who is about to face his colleagues at the Medical Association after a string of scandals that could mean the end of his career. Chekhov uses his medical training in an analytic tour-de-force, showing the doctor going through a series of mental gyrations as he prepares to leave his house for the fateful meeting.

Almost a century has passed since Chekhov's death, and it is surprising that so many of these early masterpieces have not been translated into English. As Chekhov specialist Julie de Sherbinin points out in a letter to *Harper's Magazine* (February 1998), "The gaps in English translation of his early work can be attributed to various factors: these stories were long considered products of an 'immature' writer, they are rich in colloquialisms and wordplay and thus are hard to translate, and they often depend on cultural context for their humor."

Since Chekhov's death in 1904 there have been many translations of his other prose pieces. During the Bloomsbury years, Constance Garnett established his position as an international literary figure by publishing seventeen volumes of her Chekhov translations—201 stories. The quantity of Chekhov's work was so great that Garnett had to make a selection, and her selections have subsequently remained largely uncontested. Consecutive generations of Chekhov translators have not veered far from her choice of stories, only occasionally introducing new, untranslated material.

In many of his letters throughout his life Chekhov downplayed his stories, calling them "little trifles," even "literary excrements" that were written "half-consciously." He playfully confided that he wrote things off the cuff, as if he were eating bliny. "I don't love money sufficiently for medicine, and I don't have enough passion, that is, talent, for literature." Chekhov's natural self-irony in talking about his work misled many people who knew him, and later most of his biographers; but there is evidence that behind closed doors he was always a painstakingly careful writer. His friend Nikolai Yozhov, for instance, was both shocked and amazed at catching him one day transcribing a story by Tolstoy. Chekhov told him that he often did this, that it was just an exercise—he was rewriting the story, editing it down. (Yozhov was outraged.) Chekhov wrote in an earnest letter of advice to his older brother Alexander, also a writer, "Most important of all: keep watch, observe, huff and puff, rewrite everything five times, condensing and so on, always remembering that all of Petersburg follows the work of the Chekhov brothers!"

It is a widely accepted myth that Chekhov initially saw writing as the road to a quick ruble, that he spent the first part of his career as a hack writer for the gutter press, and that it was only in midlife that he miraculously found literature. A closer look at the quality of his early work refutes this.

Thomas Mann, in an essay published in *Sinn und Form* in 1954 commemorating the fiftieth anniversary of Chekhov's death, was one of the first to point out that Chekhov's diffident public attitude toward his writing had misled subsequent generations into a distorted view of his work. "In my eyes," Mann wrote,

> the reason Chekhov has to a large extent been undervalued in Europe and even in Russia is due to his extremely sober, critical, and skeptical stance towards himself, and the dissatisfaction with which he regarded his accomplishments—in short, his modesty. This modesty was an extremely appealing trait, but it was not designed to exact respect from the world and, one could say that it set the

world a bad example. For, the view we have of ourselves is not without influence on the image that people have of us, and can taint that image and possibly adulterate it. Chekhov the short-story writer was convinced for far too long of his artistic unworthiness and the insignificance of his capabilities. It was only slowly and with great difficulty that he gained a modicum of belief in himself—the belief that cannot be absent if others are to believe in us. To the end of his life he showed no trace of the literary grand seigneur, and even less of the sage and prophet.*

Another important factor that led earlier generations of scholars to deprecate Chekhov's early work was his own selection of stories for the ten-volume *Sobranie Sochinenii* (Collected Works, 1899–1902). It was felt that the pieces Chekhov chose not to include were in his eyes not up to par. And until quite recently the general scholarly trend of thought has been to agree with him. Stories told in minimalist telegrams? Absurdist vignettes opening with "I was chased by 30 dogs, 7 of which were white"? How could one compare these wild pieces with the multilayered style of *The Cherry Orchard* or "The Lady with the Lap Dog," a style that has served as a model for many writers of the twentieth century?

* From "Versuch ueber Tschechow," by Thomas Mann, written July 15, 1954. The essay initially appeared in the German literary magazine *Sinn und Form*, and was included in Thomas Mann's *Gesammelte Werke* (S. Fischer, 1960). Excerpt translated by Peter Constantine with the permission of Alfred A. Knopf Inc.

Scholars today are taking a broader view in assessing the scope of Chekhov's early work. Pieces such as "Questions Posed by a Mad Mathematician," until recently dismissed as "scurrilous sketches" and "impenetrably vacuous balderdash," are now viewed as important experimental works. Thomas Venclova, for instance, discusses Chekhov's early prose as a major precursor of the Russian absurdist writers of the late 1920s and Eugène Ionesco.

My work on this book began two years ago in the Slavic and Baltic Division of the New York Public Library. I was looking through a heavy bound volume of *Budilnik* issues from 1880. The magazines had a very progressive, almost late Edwardian look, much like early issues of the British magazine *Punch*. The drawings were colored, which surprised me, and after the middle of 1880 the lettering on the title pages was flushed with gold. Just as I was wondering how a fin-de-siècle printer could have managed that, I noticed a short story signed "A. Chekhov"—Alexander Chekhov, Anton's older brother. In the next few issues there were more "A. Chekhov" signatures, and quite a few "Arteopod," an alias Alexander often used.

And then came the first stories by Antosha Chekhonte—Anton Chekhov.

To my surprise, the New York Public library has all the Moscow and St. Petersburg magazines in which Chekhov was first published: *Budilnik, Strekoza* (Dragonfly), *Oskolki*. As I began reading Chekhov's early stories in context, a very different image of him jumped off the page. The initial picture in my mind of the sedate literary elder with monocle and cane (the picture of Chekhov on most book covers) disappeared, and a younger, livelier, more energetic image of the writer took its place. I soon found that the New York Public Library has one of the best collections of turn-of-the-century and earlier Russian material in the world. Some of its rare books are not even available in the Russian State Library. It houses almost 400,000 books, manuscripts, and periodicals, including volumes from the libraries of twenty-six members of the Romanov dynasty—some items dating back to the fourteenth century. Avrahm Yarmolinsky, a Chekhov scholar and translator, who served as chief of the Slavic and Baltic Division, had traveled to Russia during the 1920s and 1930s, buying up the libraries of the Romanovs and the former aristocracy. It was quite an experience working on this book surrounded by such Imperial Russian treasures.

*The Undiscovered Chekhov* brings to English-speaking readers a new body of Chekhov's work that deserves a wider audience. I chose these stories as representative pieces out of the large body of Chekhov's writing spanning the period from 1880 to 1887. His work from that time is largely unknown outside Russia. Without it, one cannot have a full picture of Chekhov as a writer.

---

I have arranged the stories chronologically in order to show the direction of Chekhov's development. The second section, "This and That," brings together some of the shorter humorous vignettes that Chekhov published in magazine columns titled "This and That," "Something," or "Thoughts and Aphorisms."

In *The Undiscovered Chekhov,* one sees exuberance and energy, but also the technique of a young writer of genius. These are the stories that made Chekhov famous in his day.

## Acknowledgments

My warmest thanks to Anneta Greenlee for her scholarly input and for checking my translations. Her knowledge of nineteenth-century Russian literature and the nuances of the language of the time was invaluable. I would also like to thank the Chekhov specialist Julie de Sherbinin for her recommendations. Her advice on the fine points of Chekhov's early work were especially helpful. I am grateful to Barbara Jones, senior editor of *Harper's Magazine,* for her editorial advice on the stories that appeared in the magazine, to Linda Asher for her editorial advice on the story "On Mortality: A Carnival Tale," which appeared in the *New Yorker,* and also to Bradford Morrow, who made many extremely helpful suggestions. Edward Kasinec, chief of the Slavic and Baltic Division of the New York Public Library, and Tatiana Gizdavcic, librarian, for their help in locating often-hard-to-find material.

I am very grateful to my agent, Jessica Wainwright, who enthusiastically encouraged me, and to my editor, Dan Simon, for his help and support.

My very special thanks to Burton Pike, who inspired me to begin this project, and encouraged, helped, and advised me throughout it.

# PART
# ONE

# SARAH BERNHARDT COMES TO TOWN

TELEGRAM
Have been drinking to Sarah's health all week! Enchanting! She actually dies standing up! Our actors can't touch the Parisians! Sitting there, you feel you're in Paradise! Regards to Mankya.

Petrov

TELEGRAM
Lieutenant Egorov. Come, you can have my ticket— I'm not going again. It's just rubbish. Nothing special. A waste of money.

---

FROM DR. KLOPSON, M.D.,
TO DR. VERFLUCHTERSCHWEIN, M.D.

Dear friend. Last night I saw S.B. Her chest—paralytic and flat. Skeletal and muscular structure—unsatisfactory. Neck—so long and thin that both the venae jugulares and even the arteriae carotides are clearly visible. Her musculi sternocleido-mastoidei are barely noticeable. Sitting in second row orchestra I could detect clear signs of anemia. No cough. On stage she was all wrapped up, which led me to deduce that she must be feverish. My diagnosis: anemia and atrophia musculorum. What is quite amazing is that her lachrymal glands react to voluntary stimuli: Tears flowed from her eyes, and her nose showed signs of hyperemia whenever she was called upon to weep.

FROM NADIA N. TO KATYA H.

Dear Katya. Last night I went to the theater and saw Sera Burnyard. Oh Katya, how many diamonds that woman has! All night I cried at the thought that I'll never ever own such a heap of diamonds. (I'll tell you later all about her dress). Oh how I'd love to be Sera Burnyard! They were drinking real champagne on stage! But what was strange Katya I speak excellent French but I didn't get a word they were saying. Their French was funny. I had to sit in the gallery! That monster of mine couldn't get me a better ticket. The monster! Now

I regret I was so cold to S. on Monday, he could have got orchestra seats. S. will do anything for a kiss. Just to spite that monster, tomorrow I'll have S. get both you and me a ticket.

Your N.

FROM A NEWSPAPER EDITOR TO A REPORTER

Ivan Mikhailovitch! This is an abomination! Every evening you traipse down to the theater with a press ticket, and I have yet to see a single line about the show! What are you waiting for? Right now Sarah Bernhardt is the hottest—and we need to cover her now. For God's sake, get a move on!

Answer: I don't quite know what to write. Should I praise her? Let's see what everyone else writes—time's on our side.

Yours, K.

P.S. I'll be at the office today, get my pay ready. If you want the press tickets back, send someone over.

LETTER SENT BY MISS N. TO THE SAME REPORTER

You are a darling, Ivan Mikhailovitch! Thank you for the ticket! I have feasted my eyes on Sarah, and I absolutely insist that you praise her to the skies. Can you check with your office to see if my sister can also get a press ticket? I'll be most grateful to you.

Your N.

———

Answer: It can be done... but there will be a slight fee. The fee is minimal: permission to visit you on Saturday.

TO THE NEWSPAPER EDITOR FROM HIS WIFE

If you don't send me a ticket for Sarah Bernhardt tonight, don't bother coming home. It's quite obvious your reporters are more important to you than your own wife. I want to go to the theater!

FROM THE NEWSPAPER EDITOR TO HIS WIFE

Please, dear! Be reasonable! As it is, this whole Sarah Bernhardt business is driving me to distraction!

FROM AN USHER'S NOTEBOOK

Let in four. Fourteen rubles.

Let in five. Fifteen r.

Let in three and one madame. Fifteen rubles.

Thank God I didn't go to the theater and that I sold that ticket I had. I heard Sarah Bernhardt played in French. I wouldn't have understood a word...

Major Kovalyov

Dear Mitya! I beg of you! Can you ask your wife, tactfully, to enthuse more quietly about Sarah Bernhardt's dresses

---

when she's with us in the box? At the last performance she was whispering so loud that I couldn't hear a word of what was being said on stage. Please ask her, but tactfully. I'd be most obliged.

Your U.

FROM THE SLAVOPHILE K. TO HIS SON

My dear son. I opened my eyes and saw omens of depravity all around! Thousands of Russian Orthodox Christians heralding a union with the people— thronging to the theater to lay their gold at the feet of that Jewess... Liberals, Conservatives...!

A NOTE

Darling! When it comes to Sarah Bernhardt, as the saying goes: you can dip a frog in honey but it doesn't mean I'll eat it.

Sobakevitch

# ON THE TRAIN

THE POST TRAIN RACES full speed from the Happy-Trach-Tararach station to the Run-for-Your-Life station. The locomotive whistles, hisses, puffs, snorts; the cars shake, and their unoiled wheels howl like wolves and screech like owls! Darkness is over the skies, over the earth, and in the cars... "Something-will-happen, something-will-happen," the wagons hammer, rattling with age. "Ohohohoho!" the locomotive joins in. Pocket-friskers and cold drafts sweep through the wagons. Terrible! I stick my head out the window and look aimlessly into the endless expanse. All the lights are green, but somewhere down the line I'm sure all hell will break loose. The signal disk and the station lights are not yet visible. Darkness, anguish, thoughts of death, memories of childhood, oh God!

"I have sinned!" I whisper, "I have sinned!"

I feel a hand slip into my back pocket. The pocket is empty, but still it's horrifying. I turn round. A stranger is standing next to me. He is wearing a straw hat and a dark gray shirt.

"Can I help you?" I ask him, patting my hands over my pockets.

"No, I'm just looking out the window!" he answers, pulling back his hand and leaning against my back.

There is a powerful, ear-splitting whistle. The train slows and slows, and finally stops. I get out of the car and walk over to the station buffet for a drink to bolster my courage. The buffet is bustling with passengers and train workers.

"A vodka, sweet and easy!" the thickset chief conductor says, turning to a fat gentleman. The fat gentleman wants to say something but can't: his year-old sandwich is stuck in his throat.

"Poli-i-i-ce! Poli-i-i-ce!" someone outside on the platform is shouting, as in primordial times before the Deluge hungry mastodons, ichthyosaurs, and plesiosaurs would have bellowed. I go to see what's happening. A man with a cockade on his hat is standing outside one of the first-class cars, pointing to his feet. Someone had swiped the poor man's shoes and socks while he was sleeping.

"What am I going to do?" he shouts. "I have to go all the way to Revel! Can you believe this?"

———

A policeman, standing in front of him, informs him, "It's against the rules to shout here." I climb back into my car, number 224. It's exactly like it was: dark, the sound of snoring, tobacco, and soot in the air—the smell of Mother Russia. A red-haired inspector traveling to Kiev from Ryazan is snoring next to me... a few feet away from him a pretty girl is dozing... a peasant in a straw hat snorts, puffs, changes position, and doesn't know where to put his long legs... in the corner someone is munching, and loudly smacking his lips. Under the benches people lie in deep sleep. The door creaks. Two wrinkly little old women come hobbling in with bundles on their backs...

"Here! Let's sit here!" one of them says. "Ooh, it's dark! Temptations from Below! Oops, I stepped on someone!... But where is Pakhom?"

"Pakhom? Oh, good gracious! Where has he got to now! Oh, good gracious!"

The little old woman bustles about, opens the window, and looks up and down the platform.

"Pa-a-a-khom!" she brays. "Where are you? Pakhom! We're over here!"

"I have a pro-o-o-blem!" a voice calls from outside. "They won't let me on!"

"They won't let you on? Cowshit! No one can stop you, you have a real ticket!"

---

"They've stopped selling tickets! The ticket office is closed!"

Someone leads a horse up the platform. There is snorting, and hooves clatter.

"Get back!" the policeman shouts. "Get off immediately! Nothing but trouble!"

"Petrovna!" Pakhom moans.

Petrovna drops her bundle, takes hold of a large tin teapot, and quickly runs out of the car. The second bell rings. A little conductor with a black mustache comes in.

"You're going to have to get a ticket," he whispers to the old man sitting opposite me. "The controller just got on!"

"Really! Oh... That's bad!... What, the Prince himself?"

"The Prince? Ha, you could beat him with a stick, he'd never come to do an inspection himself."

"So, who is it? The one with the beard?"

"Yes, him."

"Well, if it's him, that's fine. He's a good man!"

"It's up to you."

"Are there many ride-hoppers today?"

"At least forty."

"I say, good for them! Fast workers!"

My heart constricts. I'm a ride-hopper too. I always hop rides. On the railroads the ride-hoppers are those passengers who prefer to "inconvenience" conductors with money rather than pay the cashier at the station. Being a ride-hopper is great, dear reader. The unwritten rule is that ride-hoppers get a 75 percent discount. Furthermore, they don't have to line up at ticket windows or take their ticket out of their pockets every few minutes, and the conductor is much more courteous to them...in a nutshell, it's the best way to travel!

"What's the point of paying whatever, whenever?" the old man mumbles. "Never! I always pay the conductor directly! The conductor needs money more than the railroad does!"

The third bell rings.

"Oh dear, oh dear!" the little old woman whines. "Where on earth is Petrovna? The third bell already! O trials and tribulations! We've lost her! We've lost her, poor dear! And her things are still here... what am I going to do with her things, with her bag! Heavens above, we've lost her!"

The little old woman thinks for a moment.

"If she can't get on, she'll need it!" she says, and throws Petrovna's bag out the window.

The train sets off for Khaldeyevo, which according to my Frum tourist guide is no more than a common grave. The controller and the chief conductor enter, carrying candles.

"Ti-i-i-ckets!" the chief conductor shouts.

The controller turns to me and the old man: "Your tickets!"

We shrink back, stoop over, rummage through our pockets, and then stare at the chief conductor, who winks at us.

---

"Get their tickets!" the controller says to the conductor, and marches on. We are saved.

"Tickets! You! Show me your ticket!" The chief conductor nudges a sleeping young man. The young man wakes up and pulls the yellow ticket out of his hat.

"Where're you going?" the controller asks, twirling the ticket in his fingers. "This isn't where we're going!"

"You blockhead, this isn't where we're going!" the chief conductor chimes in. "You got on the wrong train, you idiot! You're supposed to be heading for Zhivoderevo, and we're heading for Khaldeyevo! Here's your ticket back! You should keep your eyes open!"

The young man blinks, looks dully at the smiling crowd, and starts rubbing his eyes.

"Don't cry!" people tell him. "You'd better ask them to help you! A big lout like you, probably even married with children, howling like that!"

"Ti-i-i-ckets!" the chief conductor shouts at a farmer with a top hat.

"What?"

"Your ticket! Get a move on!"

"A ticket? You need it?"

"Your ticket!"

"I see... No, definitely, why not if you need it!" The farmer with the top hat reaches into his vest, quickly pulls out a greasy piece of paper, and hands it over to the controller.

"What are you giving me here? This is your passport! I want to see your ticket!"

"This is all I have!" the farmer answers, visibly shaken.

"How can you travel when you don't have a ticket?"

"But I've paid."

"What d'you mean you paid? Whom did you pay?"

"The c-con-conducter."

"Which conductor?

"How the devil am I supposed to know which conductor? Some conductor, it's as simple as that.... You don't need a ticket, he said, you can travel without one...so I didn't get a ticket."

"Well, we'll discuss this further at the station. Madam, your ticket!"

The door creaks, opens, and to everyone's surprise Petrovna enters.

"Oh Lord, what a hard time I had finding my compartment.... How's one supposed to tell them apart, they all look the same.... And they didn't let Pakhom get on, the snakes.... Where's my bag?"

"Oh!... Temptations from Below!... I threw it out the window for you. I thought we'd left you behind!"

"You threw it where?"

"Out the window. How was I to know?"

"Oh, thank you very much! Who told you to do that, you

———

15

old hag! May the Lord forgive me! What am I going to do? Why didn't you throw your own bag out, you bitch! It's your ugly mug you should have thrown out the window! Ohh! May both your eyes fall out!"

"You'll have to send a telegram from the next station!" the laughing crowd suggests.

Petrovna starts wailing loudly and spouting profanities. Her friend, also crying, is clutching her bag. The conductor comes in.

"Whose things are these?" he shouts, holding up Petrovna's bag.

"Pret-t-t-y!" the old man sitting opposite whispers to me, nodding his head at the pretty girl. "Mmm...pret-t-y...pity I don't have any chloroform on me! One whiff and she'd be out! Then I could kiss her for all I'm worth!"

The man in the straw hat stirs uncomfortably, and in a loud voice curses his long legs.

"Scientists," he mumbles. "Scientists... you can't fight the nature of things...scientists! Ha! How come they haven't come up with something so we can screw our legs on and off at will?"

"It's got nothing to do with me.... Speak to the public prosecutor!" the inspector sitting next to me shouts.

In the far corner two high school boys, a noncommissioned officer, and a blue-eyed young man are huddled together playing a game of cards by the light of their cigarettes.

———

A tall lady is sitting haughtily to my right. She reeks of powder and patchouli.

"Oh how absolutely divine it is to be en route!" some goose is whispering into her ear, her voice sugary... nauseatingly sugary...frenchifying her g's, n's, and r's. "One's rapprochement is never as quick and as charming as it is when one is en route. Oh, how I do love being en route!"

A kiss...another...what the hell is going on?

The pretty girl wakes up, looks around, and unconsciously rests her head against the man sitting next to her, the devotee of Justice... but the idiot is asleep.

The train stops. A halt. "The train will be stopping for two minutes!" a hoarse bass voice mutters outside the railroad car. Two minutes pass, two more.... Five minutes pass, ten, twenty, and the train is still standing. What the hell's going on! I get off the train and make my way to the locomotive.

"Ivan Matevitch! Get a move on! Damn!" the chief conductor shouts from the locomotive.

The engine driver crawls out from under the locomotive, red, wet, a piece of soot sticking to his nose...

"Damn you! Damn you!" he shouts up at the chief conductor. "Get off my back! Are you blind? Can't you see what's going on? God! Aaah... I wish you'd all go to hell! This is supposed to be a locomotive? This is no locomotive, it's a pile of junk! I'm not traveling any farther on this!"

———

"What're we going to do?"

"You can do whatever you like! How about getting another locomotive—I refuse to travel on this one! Don't you understand?"

The driver's helpers run around the broken-down engine, banging, shouting... the station chief in a red cap tells his assistant Jewish jokes...it starts to rain...I head back to my railroad car...the stranger in the straw hat and the dark gray shirt rushes by...he's carrying a suitcase. God...it's my suitcase!

---

# THE TRIAL

THE HUT OF KUZMA Egorov, the shopkeeper. Hot and stifling. Damned mosquitoes and flies buzz near eyes and ears, a real nuisance. There's a cloud of tobacco smoke, yet it doesn't smell of tobacco but of salted fish. A heaviness hangs in the air, on everyone's faces, in the buzzing of the mosquitoes.

There is a large table and on it scissors, a jar with a greenish ointment, a saucer filled with walnut shells, paper bags, empty bottles. Seated around the table are Kuzma Egorov himself, Theophan Manafuilov the village priest, Ivanov the medical assistant, the village elder, Mikhailo the bass, Parfenti Ivanovitch the godfather, and Fortunatov, a policeman from town who is visiting Aunt Anise. At a respectful distance from the table stands Kuzma Egorov's son, Seraphion, who is apprenticed to a barber in town and has come home for the holidays. Seraphion feels very uneasy, and with a trembling hand fidgets with his mustache. Kuzma Egorov's hut also serves provisionally as a medical "station," and out in the hall the ill have gathered: just now they brought in an old woman with a broken rib. She is lying there moaning, waiting for the medical assistant to finally grace her with his attention. Outside by the window a crowd has gathered to see Kuzma Egorov give his son a flogging.

"You keep saying that I'm lying," Seraphion says to his father, "which is why I intend to keep things short. We are in the nineteenth century, Father. Words are meaningless, because theories, as you yourself surely know, simply can't exist without some practical basis."

"Shut up!" Kuzma Egorov sternly shouts. "Don't change the subject; just give me the meat and potatoes. What have you done with my money?"

"Your money? But... surely, you yourself must be clever enough to see that I would never have touched your money. After all, you're not hoarding it for me... I would never be tempted!"

"Be frank with us, Seraphion Kuzmitch!" the village priest exclaims. "Why do you think we are questioning you? We want to set you on the straight and narrow path to righteousness. Your father only wants what is good for you.... So he

---

asked us over.... You must be frank with us.... Did you sin? Was it you who took the twenty-five rubles lying in your father's chest of drawers, or wasn't it?

Seraphion spits into the corner and says nothing.

"Answer!" Kuzma Egorov shouts, banging his fist on the table. "Was it you or wasn't it?"

"Fine, have it your way, say it was me who took it! But there is no point in shouting, Father! No point in banging your fist till the table breaks into a thousand pieces! I have never taken your money, and if I did it was out of necessity... I am a living person, an animated noun, and I need money. I am not a rock!"

"Go earn yourself as much money as you need, then you won't have to rob me blind. You're not the only one in this family! There are six others!"

"I am fully aware of that, but due to the weakness of my health, as you know, I find it difficult to earn money. And how you can reproach me for nothing more than a piece of bread, you will have to answer to the Lord God himself...

"Oh, weakness of health, is it? What's so difficult about being a barber? All you have to do is cut a bit here and a bit there, and even that's too much for you!"

"You call that a job? It's not a job, it's a feeble excuse for a job. With my education I can't work in such circumstances!"

"You aren't reasoning correctly, Seraphion Kuzmitch!" the village priest says. "Your job is honorable, noble. After all, you

---

work in the biggest town in the province, and you shave and barber noble, highbrow people. Even generals need your services."

"Ha! I can tell you a thing or two about generals."

The medical assistant is slightly tipsy: "According to my medical opinion," he says, "you are turpentine and nothing else!"

"We know your medicine!... Who, if I may ask, mistook the drunk carpenter for a corpse last year and almost dissected him? If he hadn't woken up, you would have cut his stomach open. And who, may I ask, always mixes castor oil with hempseed oil?"

"That's medicine for you!"

"And who sent Malanya to kingdom come? You administered laxatives and then constipators, and then laxatives again, and she finally broke down. It's not people you should be treating but, pardon my frankness, dogs!"

"May Malanya rest in peace," Kuzma Egorov says. "May she rest in peace. It wasn't she who took the money, it's not her we're talking about...by the way, you didn't give the money to that Alonya, did you?"

"Alonya! Shame on you to speak that woman's name in front of a policeman and a man of the cloth!"

"So out with it! Did you take the money or didn't you?"

The village elder hobbles out from behind the table, lights

a match by striking it over his knee, and deferentially holds it up to the policeman's pipe.

"Damn!" the policeman shouts. "You filled my nose with powder!"

Puffing on his pipe, he gets up from the table, walks up to Seraphion, and maliciously looking him in the eye, shouts in a shrill voice: "Who the hell are you? What is this? Why! Huh? What does all this mean? Why don't you answer the question? Insubordination? Taking someone's money like that! Shut up! Answer! Speak! Answer!"

"If..."

"Shut up!"

"If you could... be just a little quieter! If... You don't scare me! Who do you think you are! You—you're just an idiot, it's as simple as that! If my father wishes to throw me to the dogs, then so be it!... Go on, torture me! Beat me!"

"Shut up! No conversation! I can see right through you! Are you a thief? What are you? Shut up! Do you know who I am? No debates!"

"Punishment is inevitable," the village priest sighs. "When criminals don't ease their guilt with a confession, then, Kuzma Egorov, flogging is inevitable. My conclusion is: it's inevitable!"

"Whip him!" Mikhailo the bass says, in such a thundering baritone that everyone jumps.

"For the last time: Was it you, yes or no?"

———

23

"If this is what you want... fine... You can flog me! I am ready!"

"You will be flogged!" Kuzma Egorov resolves, and he rises from the table, blood rushing to his neck.

The crowd outside pushes closer to the window. In the hall the sick flock to the door, trying to peek in. Even the old woman with the broken rib is craning her head.

"Bend over!" Kuzma Egorov says.

Seraphion tears off his jacket, crosses himself, and calmly bends over the bench.

"You may flog me," he says.

Kuzma Egorov picks up the strap, looks into the crowd for a few seconds as if waiting for someone to help him, and then begins.

"One! Two! Three!" Mikhailo counts in a deep bass. "Eight! Nine!"

The village priest stands in the corner, leafing through his book with lowered eyes.

"Twenty! Twenty-one!"

"Enough!" Kuzma Egorov says.

"More!" whispers Fortunatov the policeman. "More! More! Give it to him!"

"My conclusion is: definitely a few more!" the village priest says, looking up from his book.

"He didn't even wince!" the people outside mutter.

———

The sick people in the hall make way, and Kuzma Egorov's wife enters the room, her starched dress crackling.

"Kuzma!" she says to her husband. "What's this money I found in your pocket? Isn't it the money you were just looking for?"

"Oh, it is! Seraphion, get up, we've found the money! I put it in my pocket yesterday and forgot all about it!"

"More!" Fortunatov mumbles. "He must be beaten! Give it to him!"

"We found the money! Get up!"

Seraphion gets up, puts his jacket on, and sits down at the table. Drawn-out silence. Embarrassed, the village priest blows his nose in his handkerchief.

"Forgive me," Kuzma Egorov mumbles, turning to his son. "Well, you know, damn! Who would have thought we'd find it just like that?"

"It's all right. After all it's not the first time.... Please don't worry. I am always ready to suffer any torment."

"Have a drink... it'll help heal the wounds."

Seraphion drinks, lifts his bluish nose high into the air, and with a heroic flourish walks out of the hut. For a long time afterward Fortunatov the policeman paces up and down the courtyard, his face red, his eyes goggling, muttering:

"More! More! Give it to him!"

———

# CONFESSION— OR OLYA, ZHENYA, ZOYA: A LETTER

MA CHÉRE, YOU ASKED me, among other things, in your sweet letter, my dear unforgettable friend, why, although I am thirty-nine years old, I have to this day never married.

My dear friend, I hold family life in the highest possible esteem. I never married simply because goddamn Fate was not propitious. I set out to get married a good fifteen times, but did not manage to because everything in this world—and particularly in my life—seems to hinge on chance. Everything depends on it! Chance, that despot! Let me cite a few incidents thanks to which I still lead a contemptibly lonely life.

## *First Incident*

It was a delightful June morning. The sky was as clear as the clearest Prussian blue. The sun played on the waters of the river and brushed the dewy grass with its rays. The river and the meadow were strewn with rich diamonds of light. The birds were singing, as if with one voice. We walked down the path of yellowish sand, and with happy hearts drank in the sweet aromas of the June morning. The trees looked upon us so gently, and whispered all kinds of nice—I'm sure—and tender things. Olya Gruzdofska's hand (she's now married to the son of your chief of police) lay in mine, and her tiny little finger kept brushing over my thumb.... Her cheeks glowed, and her eyes... O ma chére, what exquisite eyes! There was so much charm, truth, innocence, joyousness, childish naïveté, in those blue sparkling eyes of hers! I fell in love with her blond braids, and with the little footprints her tiny feet left in the sand.

"I have devoted my life, Olga Maksimovna, to science!" I whispered, terrified that her little finger would slip off my thumb. "The future will bring with it a professorial chair... on my conscience there are questions... scientific ones... my life is filled with hard work, troubles, lofty... I mean... well, basically, I'm going to be a professor... I am an honest man, Olga Maksimovna... I'm not rich, but... I need someone who with her presence...(Olya blushed and shyly lowered her eyes; her little finger was trembling) who with her presence... Olya! Look up at the sky! Look how pure it is... my life is just as boundlessly pure!"

My tongue didn't have time to scramble out of this quagmire of drivel: Olya suddenly lifted her head, snatched her hand away from mine, and clapped her palms together. A flock of geese with little goslings was waddling towards us. Olya ran over to them and, laughing out loud, stretched her arms toward them.... O what beauteous arms, ma chére!

"Squawk, squawk, squawk!" the geese called out, craning their necks, peering at Olya from the side.

"Here goosey-goose, here goosey-goose!" Olya shouted, and reached out to touch a little gosling.

The gosling was quite bright for its age. It ran from Olya's approaching fingers straight to its daddy, a very large foolish-looking gander, and seemed to complain to him. The gander spread his wings. Naughty Olya reached out to touch some other goslings. At that moment something terrible happened: the gander lowered his neck to the ground and, hissing like a snake, marched fiercely toward Olya. Olya squealed and retreated, the gander close at her heels. Olya looked back, squealed even louder, and went completely white. Her pretty, girlish face was twisted with terror and despair. It was as if she were being chased by three hundred devils.

I rushed to help her and banged the gander on the head

---

with my walking stick. The damn gander still managed to quickly snap at the hem of her dress. With wide eyes and terror-stricken face, trembling all over, Olya fell into my arms.

"You're such a coward!" I said to her.

"Thrash that goose!" she moaned, and burst into tears.

Suddenly I no longer saw naïveté or childishness in her frightened little face—but idiocy! Ma chére, I cannot abide faintheartedness! I cannot imagine being married to a fainthearted, cowardly woman!

The gander ruined everything. After calming Olya down, I went home. I couldn't get that expression of hers—cowardly to the point of idiocy—out of my mind. In my eyes, Olya had lost all her charm. I dropped her.

## Second Incident

As you know, my friend, I am a writer. The gods ignited within my breast the sacred flame, and I have seen it as my duty to take up the pen! I am a high priest of Apollo! Every beat of my heart, every breath I take, in short—I have sacrificed everything on the altar of my muse. I write and I write and I write... take away my pen, and I'm dead! You laugh! You do not believe me! I swear most solemnly that it is true!

But as you surely know, ma chére, this world of ours is a bad place for art. The world is big and bountiful, but a writer can find no place for himself in it! A writer is an eternal orphan, an exile, a scapegoat, a defenseless child! I divide mankind into two categories: writers and enviers! The former write, and the latter die of jealousy and spend all their time plotting and scheming against them. I have always fallen prey, and always will, to these plotters! They have ruined my life! They have taken over the writing business, calling themselves editors and publishers, striving with all their might to ruin us writers! Damn them!

Anyway.... For a while I was courting Zhenya Pshikova. You must remember her, that sweet, dreamy, black-haired girl... she's now married to your neighbor, Karl Ivanovitch Wanze (á propos, in German Wanze means "bedbug." But please don't tell Zhenya, she'd be very upset). Zhenya was in love with the writer within me. She believed in my calling as deeply as I did. She cherished my hopes. But she was so young! She had not yet grasped the aforementioned division of humanity into two categories! She did not believe in this division! She did not believe it, and one fine day...catastrophe!

I was staying at the Pshikovs' dacha. The family looked on me as the groom-to-be and Zhenya as the bride. I wrote—she read. What a critic she was, ma chére! She was as objective as Aristides and as stern as Cato. I dedicated my works to her. One of these pieces she really liked. She wanted to see it in print, so I sent it to one of the magazines. I sent

---

it on the first of July and waited two weeks for the answer. The fifteenth of July came, and Zhenya and I finally received the letter we had been waiting for. We opened it; she went red, I went white. Beneath the address the following was written: "Shlendovo village, Mr. M. B. You don't have a drop of talent in you. God knows what the hell you're writing about. Please don't waste your stamps and our time! Find yourself another occupation!"

Ridiculous... it was obvious that a bunch of idiots had written this.

"I see..." Zhenya mumbled.

"The damn... swine!" I muttered. So, ma chére Yevgenia Markovna, are you still smiling at my division of the world into writers and enviers?

Zhenya thought for a while and then yawned.

"Well," she said, "maybe you don't have any talent after all. They surely know best. Last year Fyodor Fyodosevitch spent the whole summer fishing by the river with me. All you do is write, write, write! It's so boring!"

Well! How do you like that! After all those sleepless nights we spent together, I writing, she reading! With both of us sacrificing ourselves to my muse! Ha!

Zhenya cooled to my writing, and by extension to me. We broke up. It had to be.

---

## Third Incident

You know, of course, my dear unforgettable friend, that I am a fervent music lover. Music is my passion, my true element. The names Mozart, Beethoven, Chopin, Mendelssohn, Gounod, are not the names of men—they are the names of giants! I love classical music. I scorn operettas, as I scorn vaudeville! I am a true habitué of the opera. Our stars Khokhlov, Kochetova, Barzal, Usatov, Korsov... are simply wonderful people! How I regret that I do not know any singers personally. Were I to know one, I would bare my soul in humble gratitude!

Last winter I went to the opera particularly often. I did not go alone—I went with the Pepsinov family. It is such a pity that you do not know this dear family! Each winter the Pepsinovs book a loge. They are devoted to music, heart and soul. The crown of this dear family is Colonel Pepsinov's daughter Zoya. What a girl, my dear friend! Her pink lips alone could drive someone like me out of his mind! She is shapely, beautiful, clever. I loved her... I loved her madly, passionately, terribly! My blood was boiling when I sat next to her. You smile, ma chére? You can smile! You cannot comprehend the love a writer feels! A writer's love is—Mount Etna coupled with Mount Vesuvius! Zoya loved me. Her eyes always rested on my eyes, which were constantly seeking out her eyes. We were happy. It was but one step to marriage.

---

But we foundered.

Faust was playing. Faust, my dear friend, was written by Gounod, and Gounod is one of the greatest musicians on earth. On the way to the theater, I decided to declare my love to Zoya during the first act. I have never understood that act—it was a mistake on the part of the great Gounod to have written that first act!

The opera began. Zoya and I slipped out to the foyer. She sat next to me and, shivering with expectation and happiness, nervously fanned herself. How beautiful she looked in the glittering lights, ma chére, how terribly beautiful!

"The overture," I began my declaration, "led me to some reflections, Zoya Egorovna... so much feeling, so much... you listen and you long... you long for, well, for that something, and you listen..."

I hiccupped, and continued:

"You long for something... special! You long for something unearthly... Love? Passion? Yes... it must be...love (I hiccupped). Yes, love!"

Zoya smiled in confusion, and fanned herself harder. I hiccupped. I can't stand hiccups!

"Zoya Egorovna! Tell me, I beg of you! Do you know this feeling? (I hiccupped.) Zoya Egorovna! I am trembling for your answer!"

"I... I... don't understand..."

———

"Sorry, that was just a hiccup... It'll pass... I'm talking about that all-embracing feeling that... damn!"

"Have some water!"

I'll make my declaration, and then I'll quickly go down to the buffet, I thought to myself, and continued:

"In a nutshell, Zoya Egorovna... you, of course, will have noticed..."

I hiccupped, and then in my consternation bit my tongue.

"You will, of course, have noticed (I hiccupped)... you've known me almost a year now... well... I'm an honest man, Zoya Egorovna! I am a hardworking man! I am not rich, it's true, but..."

I hiccupped and leaped up.

"I think you should have some water!" Zoya suggested. I moved a few steps away from the sofa, tapped my finger on my throat, and hiccupped again. Ma chére, I was in a terrible predicament! Zoya stood up, and marched off to the loge with me close on her heels. After escorting her, I hiccupped and quickly ran off to the buffet. I drank five or six glasses of water, and the hiccups seemed somehow to quiet down. I smoked a cigarette and returned to the loge. Zoya's brother got up and gave me his seat, the seat next to my darling Zoya. I sat down, and at that very moment... hiccupped! About five minutes passed, I hiccupped, hiccupped somehow strangely, with a wheeze. I got up and went to stand by the loge door. It is bet-

---

ter, ma chére, to hiccup by a door than into the ear of the woman one loves! I hiccupped. A schoolboy from the loge next to ours looked at me and laughed out loud. The joy with which that little brute laughed! And the joy with which I would have gladly ripped the horrible little brat's ear off! He laughed as they were singing the great "Faust" aria on stage! What blasphemy! No, ma chére! As children we would never have comported ourselves in this manner! Cursing the impertinent schoolboy, I hiccupped again.... Laughter broke out in the neighboring loges.

"Encore!" the schoolboy loudly whispered.

"What the hell!" Colonel Pepsinov mumbled. "Couldn't you have hiccupped at home, sir?"

Zoya went red. I hiccupped one last time and, furiously clenching my fists, ran out of the loge. I started walking up and down the corridor. I walked and walked and walked—hiccupping constantly. I ate, I drank, I tried everything—finally at the beginning of the fourth act I gave up and went home. The moment I unlocked the door, as if to spite me, my hiccups stopped. I slapped my neck, and shouted:

"Go on, hiccup! Now you can hiccup all you want, you poor, booed-off fiancé! No, you were not booed off, you were hiccupped off!"

The following day I went to visit the Pepsinovs the way I always did. Zoya didn't come down for dinner, and sent word that she couldn't see me as she wasn't feeling well, while

―――――

Pepsinov spoke at length about certain young people who didn't know how to comport themselves in public. The fool! He's obviously not aware that the organs that induce hiccupping are not subject to voluntary stimuli! Stimuli, ma chére, means "shakers."

"Would you give your daughter—that is, if you had one—to a man who wouldn't think twice about belching in public?" Pepsinov asked me after dinner. "Ha? Well?"

"Um, yes... I would," I muttered.

"Quite a mistake!"

That was the end of Zoya as far as I was concerned. She could not forgive my hiccupping. For her that was the end of me. Would you like me to describe the remaining twelve incidents?

I could, but... enough is enough! The veins on my temples have swollen, tears are flowing freely, and my liver is churning.... "O brother writers, our destiny doth weave fateful threads!" I wish you, ma chére, all the very best! I squeeze your hand tightly, and send my warmest regards to Paul. I hear that he is a good husband and father. God bless him! Pity, though, that he drinks so heavily (this, by the way, ma chére, is not a reproach!).

All the very best, ma chére. Your faithful servant, Baldastov.

---

# VILLAGE DOCTORS

THE VILLAGE HOSPITAL.
Morning.

As the doctor is absent, out hunting with the district police officer, his assistants Kuzma Egorov and Gleb Glebitch are seeing patients. There are about thirty of them. Kuzma Egorov is having a cup of chicory coffee in the reception room, waiting for the sick to sign in. Gleb Glebitch, who hasn't bathed or combed his hair since the day he was born, is leaning with chest and stomach over the table, swearing and registering patients. Registration is set up like a census: the patient's name, father's name, family name, profession, place of residence, literate or illiterate, age—and then after the checkup, the diagnosis and the medicine issued.

"Damn this pen!" Gleb Glebitch shouts as he scrawls large ugly letters into the big book. "This is supposed to be ink? It's tar, not ink! The council never ceases to amaze me! They expect you to sign up patients, and then they give you two kopecks a year for ink! Next!"

A peasant with a bandaged face and baritone Mikhailo come in.

"Who are you?"

"Ivan Mikulov."

"Huh? What? Speak Russian!"

"Ivan Mikulov."

"Ivan Mikulov! I'm not talking to you! Get out! You! Your name!"

Mikhailo smiles.

"Like you don't know my name!" he says.

"What's so funny? Damn it! I've no time for jokes! Time is money, and these people come here to joke! Your name!"

"Like you don't know my name! Are you out of your mind?"

"Of course I know your name, but I still have to ask! That's the protocol... and no, I'm not mad, I don't hit the bottle like you do. I don't go in for heavy drinking, thank you very much! Name and father's name!"

"If you're so busy, why am I standing here talking to you when you already know all the answers? You've known me for five years...and now in the sixth you forget who I am?"

"I haven't forgotten, it's protocol! Do you understand? Or don't you speak Russian? Protocol!"

"Well, if it is protocol, then, whatever! So write: Mikhailo Fedotitch Izmuchenko!"

"It's not Izmuchenko, it's Izmuchenkov."

"Fine, Izmuchenkov... whatever, as long as I get cured. You can write Monkeyshine Ivanov for all I care."

"Your profession."

"Baritone."

"Your age?"

"How the hell should I know? I wasn't baptized, so I have no idea."

"Forty?"

"Could be, but then again, who knows? Write down whatever you think best."

Gleb Glebitch looks intently at Mikhailo and writes thirty-seven. Then, having given it more thought, he crosses out thirty-seven and writes forty-one.

"Literate?"

"Have you ever heard of a singer who can't read? Use your brains!"

"In front of others you have to show me a little respect and refrain from shouting at me, do you hear? Next! Who are you, what's your name?"

———

"Mikifor Pugolov, from Khaplov."

"We don't treat Khaplovites here. Next!"

"Please, have pity, Your Excellency! I had to walk twenty versts!"

"We don't treat Khaplovites! Next! Who's next! No smoking here!"

"I'm not smoking, Gleb Glebitch!"

"So what are you holding there?"

"It's my cut-off finger, Gleb Glebitch!"

"I thought it was a cigar! We don't treat Khaplovites! Next!"

Gleb Glebitch finishes registering patients. Kuzma Egorov gulps down his coffee, and is ready to begin. Gleb Glebitch takes on the role of pharmacist and goes into the drug pantry, and Kuzma Egorov takes on the medical role and slips into an oilskin apron.

"Marya Zaplakskina!" Kuzma Egorov calls out from the book.

A little old woman comes in, wrinkled and hunched over as if crushed by fate. She crosses herself and bows with deference to the medicine man.

"Yes! Shut the door! What's wrong with you?"

"My head, Mr. Doctor."

"Your whole head, or just half of it?"

"My whole head, Mr. Doctor, the whole of it!"

---

"Don't wrap your head up like that! Take that rag off! Heads must always be cold, legs warm, and your body at middling climate! Any discomfort in the stomach?"

"Oh, lots of it!"

"So... Pull down your lower eyelid. Good, that's enough. You're anemic. I'll give you some pills. Take ten of them morning, noon, and night."

Kuzma Egorov sits down and writes out the prescription.

Three grams of Liquor ferri from the bottle by the window,
as for the one on the shelf, Ivan Yakovlitch forbade us to
dispense without his permission, ten pills three times a day
for Marya Zaplakskina.

The little old woman asks what to take the pills with, bows, and leaves. Kuzma Egorov throws the prescription through a little window in the wall separating the drug pantry, and calls in the next patient.

"Timofei Stukotey!"

"Present!"

Stukotey walks in, thin and tall with a large head, from a distance resembling a knobbed walking stick.

"What's wrong with you?"

"My heart, Kuzma Egorov."

"Where?"

Stukotey points to his stomach.

"I see... how long have you felt this pain?"

"Since Holy Week... The other day I was walking and had to sit down more than ten times... I get chills, Kuzma Egorov... and then fever comes, Kuzma Egorov!"

"Hm... does anything else hurt?"

"To be honest with you, Kuzma Egorov, I hurt all over. But just cure my heart and don't worry about the rest—I'll get the old village women to cure that. I'd like you to give me some alcohol or something to stop the illness reaching my heart. These things just go up and up till they reach your heart, and when they get there, when they reach it... yes... then... uh... it snatches at your spine... and then your head feels like a stone... and then you cough!"

"Appetite?"

"None at all..."

Kuzma Egorov walks up to Stukotey and prods him, pressing his fist against his stomach.

"Did that hurt?"

"Oh...oh...uh... yes!

"How about this?"

"Oooh... unbearable!"

Kuzma Egorov asks him a few more questions, thinks for a while, and then calls Gleb Glebitch. A consultation begins.

"Stick out your tongue!" Gleb Glebitch orders.

———

The patient opens his mouth wide and sticks out his tongue.

"Farther!"

"It can't go any farther, Gleb Glebitch."

"There is no such a thing as 'can't' in this world!"

Gleb Glebitch looks at the patient intently, thinks very hard, shrugs his shoulders, and walks out of the consultation room.

"It must be a catarrh!" he shouts from the drug pantry.

"We'll give him some castor oil and some spirits of ammonia!" Kuzma Egorov shouts back. "Rub it over your stomach every morning and evening! Next!"

The patient leaves the room and goes to the pantry window in the corridor. Gleb Glebitch pours a third of a teacup of castor oil and gives it to Stukotey. He drinks it slowly, purses his lips, closes his eyes, and rubs his fingers together as if asking for something to eat that will cover the taste.

"Here's some alcohol for you!" Gleb Glebitch shouts, giving him a little bottle with ammonium chloride. "Rub this over your stomach with a rag every morning and evening. And bring back that bottle when you finish with it. Hey, don't lean on that! Go away now!"

Father Grigori's cook comes up to the window, grinning, holding her shawl over her mouth.

"How may I be of service?" Gleb Glebitch asks her.

"Lizaveta Grigoryevna sends her regards, Gleb Glebitch, and asks if she can have some mint pastilles."

"That goes without saying! For magnificent individuals of the female sex I will do anything!"

Gleb Glebitch reaches up to the shelf with a stick, and half its contents come tumbling down into Pelageya's apron.

"Tell her that Gleb Glebitch was bubbling over with enchantment as he handed you these pastilles. Did she receive my letter?"

"Yes, she got it and tore it up. Lizaveta Grigoryevna has no time for love."

"The harlot! Tell her from me she's a harlot!"

"Mikhailo Izmuchenkov!" Kuzma Egorov calls out. Baritone Mikhailo walks into the consulting room.

"Greetings, Mikhailo Fedotitch! What is wrong with you?"

"My throat, Kuzma Egorov! I came to you, as a matter of fact, so that you, to be perfectly honest with you, concerning my health, which... you see it's not a question of pain as much as it is of loss... when I'm ill, I can't sing, and the church conductor deducts forty kopecks for every mass. For yesterday's evening service he knocked off a twenty-fiver, and today for the squire's funeral the singers are getting three rubles—and me, as long as I'm sick, I get nothing. And, to be perfectly honest with you, as far as my throat is concerned it's scratching and wheezing for all it's worth—as if some

---

46

kind of a cat were in there, its paws going... scratch... scratch!"

"Could it be from your drinking hot liquids?"

"Who knows where I got this illness from! But, to be per- fectly honest with you, I can certify that hot liquid affects tenors, never baritones. When a baritone drinks, Kuzma Egorov, his voice grows richer, more imposing... it's a cold that usually affects baritones more."

Gleb Glebitch sticks his head through the pantry window.

"What should I give the old woman?" he asks. "The Liquor ferri that was by the window is gone. I'll give her the pills that are on the shelf."

"No, no! Ivan Yakovlitch forbade us to hand those out! He'll be furious!"

"So what am I supposed to give her?"

"Whatever!"

For Gleb Glebitch, "whatever" meant bicarbonate of soda.

"You shouldn't be drinking hot liquids."

"As it is, it's been three days since I've had anything... my cold is so bad... the thing is, vodka increases a baritone's hoarseness, but hoarseness deepens a baritone's voice, Kuzma Egorov, which as you know is better... without vodka there is no music... what kind of a singer would I be if I didn't drink vodka? I would not be a singer, but, to be perfectly honest with you, a joke!... If it were not for my

----

47

profession I wouldn't touch a drop of vodka. Vodka is Satan's blood!"

"Fine! I'll give you some powder that you can mix in a bottle and gargle with, once in the morning and once in the evening."

"Can I swallow it, too?"

"Yes, you can."

"Excellent. It would be bothersome if I couldn't swallow it. You gargle and gargle... and then you have to spit it out— such a waste! Then there was another thing that, to be perfectly honest with you, I wanted to ask you... you see, I have a weak stomach, and so every month I let some blood and take some herbs. Can I, in my condition, enter into a lawful marriage?"

Kuzma Egorov thinks for a while, and then says:

"No, I would advise against it."

"Oh, I'm so grateful to you! You are truly a great healer, Kuzma Egorov! Better than any doctor! By God, how many people owe their lives to you! Ooooh! More than you can count!"

Kuzma Egorov modestly lowers his eyes and boldly writes "Natri bicarbonici"—that is, bicarbonate of soda.

# AN UNSUCCESSFUL VISIT

A DANDY ENTERS A HOUSE in which he has never been before. He is paying a social call. In the hall he is met by a girl of about sixteen, wearing a cotton dress and little white apron.

"Are they home?" he asks her brazenly.

"Yes, they are."

"Hm... my little peach! So, and is the missus at home too?"

"Yes, she is," the girl answers, blushing for some reason.

"Hm... you pretty thing, you! You little vixen! Where can I leave my hat?"

"Anywhere would be fine. Please don't! Really!..."

"Come on! What are you blushing for! Hey! I won't bite you!" And the young man slaps the girl's waist with his glove.

---

"Hey, not bad!  So go ahead, announce me!"

The girl turns poppy red and runs off.

"She's young!" he decides, and walks through to the drawing room.  There he meets the lady of the house.  They sit down, chat...

About five minutes later the girl with the little apron enters the room.

"May I introduce my eldest daughter," the lady of the house says, pointing at the girl's cotton dress.

Tableau vivant.

# A HYPNOTIC SEANCE

THE LARGE HALL WAS LIT with torches and bursting with people. In the center was the hypnotist. Despite his scrawny, unprepossessing physique, he shone, glowed, and sparkled. People smiled, applauded, obeyed his every order; everyone turned pale in his presence.

He literally performed miracles. Some people he hypnotized, some he paralyzed, others he had balancing on chairs by their necks and heels; he tied a thin, tall journalist into a knot. In a word, he did whatever he pleased. He had an especially strong effect on the ladies. One glance from him and they dropped like flies. Oh, women's nerves! If it weren't for these nerves, how boring life would be!

---

Having exercised his demonic art on everyone else, the hypnotist came over to me.

"You seem to be of a suggestive nature," he said. "You are so nervous, so overwrought... wouldn't you like to take a nap?"

Why not? With pleasure, my good man, let's try. I sat down on a chair in the middle of the hall. The hypnotist sat on another chair facing me, took hold of my hands, and gazed into my eyes with his terrifying snakelike glare.

The audience surrounded us.

"Shh! Please, ladies and gentlemen! Shh... quiet!"

Silence falls. He and I sit staring at each other. A minute passes, two... Shivers run down my spine, my heart pounds, but I'm not in the least tired!

We keep sitting there. Five minutes pass, seven minutes...

"He's not giving in!" somebody shouted. "Bravo! Good man!"

We sit, we stare. I'm not tired, not even drowsy.... A local council session would have put me to sleep long ago. The audience starts whispering and sniggering. The hypnotist is distracted, and his eyes flicker. Poor man! Nobody likes losing! Save him, O spirits! Come to my eyelids, O Morpheus!

"He's not giving in!" the same voice shouted. "That's enough! Let it be! I said right away that these are nothing but conjuring tricks!"

———

Then, just as I heard my friend's voice in the crowd and moved to get up, my hand felt a strange object in its palm. My sense of touch responding, I realized that the object was a piece of paper. My father was a doctor, and doctors can sniff out a bank note at a touch. According to Darwin's theory, I must have inherited this superb faculty, along with many other talents, from my father. The bill, I could tell, was a five-ruble note, so I immediately nodded off.

"Bravo! Bravo!"

The doctors present in the hall rushed up, walked around me, prodded me, and proclaimed: "Hmm, yes... he's asleep...."

The hypnotist, pleased at his success, waved his hands over my head, and I, in a trance, began walking about the room.

"Tetanize his arm!" someone suggested.

"Yes, can you do that? Can you paralyze his arm?"

The hypnotist (not a timid man!) pulled at my right arm and started doing his machinations over it: rubbing it, blowing on it, slapping it. But my arm wouldn't obey. It just hung there dangling, and refused to become rigid.

"He's not tetanized! Wake him up! This is dangerous! He's a sensitive, high-strung boy!"

Suddenly my other palm, the left one, felt a five-ruble note brush against it. A reflex shot from my left hand to my right, and miraculously my arm went rigid.

"Bravo! Look how rigid and cold his hand is! Like a corpse!"

"We have full anesthesia, the lowering of bodily temperature and weakening of the pulse," the hypnotist announced.

The doctors checked my wrist.

"Yes, his pulse is still weak," one of them remarked.

"We have complete rigidity. His temperature is much lower..."

"How do you explain it?" one of the ladies asked.

A doctor shrugged his shoulders portentously, sighed, and said, "All we can give you is the facts! Rational explanations? Alas, there are none!"

You have the facts, and I have two fivers in my pocket, and all thanks to hypnotism—I don't need any rational explanations! Poor hypnotist! It was just your luck to tangle with a viper like me!

P.S.: Damn, what a mess!

It was only afterward that I realized it wasn't the hypnotist but my boss, Peter Fedorovitch, who slipped me the five-ruble bills.

"I did it to test your honesty," he told me.

Damn.

"This is terrible," Peter Fedorovitch said.

"Disgraceful.... I would never have expected this from you!"

———

"But sir, I have children! A wife... a mother... and things are so expensive nowadays!"

"This is disgusting! And you want to publish your own newspaper... you who cry at sentimental dinner speeches... A disgrace!... I thought you were an honest man, and it turns out that you... you are worse than... haben Sie gewesen!"

So I had to return the two fivers. What else could I do? One's reputation is, after all, more precious than money.

"It's not you I'm angry at!" my boss said. "You can go to hell for all I care—that's what you're like! But how could she have fallen into the same trap! She, of all people! She who is so gentle, so innocent, all rice pudding! She was tempted by money too! She 'fell asleep' too!"

By "she," my boss was referring to his wife, Matryona Nikolayevna...

———

# THE CROSS

THE POET ENTERS THE drawing room filled with people.

"Well," the hostess turns to him, "how did your dear little poem do? Did they print it? Was there an honorarium?"

"Oh, don't ask.... I got a cross!"

"You were awarded a cross? You, a poet? I didn't know poets were awarded crosses."

The host shakes his hand. "My sincerest congratulations! Is it a Stanislav cross or a St. Anne medal? I am so happy for you... so happy... is it a Stanislav?"

"No, a red cross!"

"Oh, you sacrificed your honorarium in aid of the Red Cross!"

"I didn't sacrifice anything!"

"The medal will definitely suit you. Do show it to us!"

The poet reaches into his side pocket and takes out his manuscript.

"Here it is!"

Everyone looks at the manuscript and sees a large red cross... but it's not the kind of cross you can pin on your lapel.

# THE CAT

BARBARA PETROVNA WOKE UP and listened. Her face went white, her large black eyes became even larger and burned with terror, when she realized she wasn't dreaming. She covered her face in horror, raised herself on her elbow, and woke her husband. Her husband curled up and, gently snoring, breathed onto her shoulder.

"Alyosha, darling! Wake up! Sweetheart! Oh, how awful!"

Alyosha stopped snoring and stretched his legs. Barbara Petrovna prodded his cheek. He stretched, sighed deeply, and woke up.

"Alyosha, darling! Wake up—someone's crying!"

"Who's crying? You're just imagining things!"

"Listen! Can't you hear? Someone's moaning.... Someone

must have left a baby on our doorstep! Oh, I can't bear the sound!"

Alyosha raised himself up and listened. Outside the wide-open window the night was gray. Along with the fragrance of lilacs and the quiet whispering of the lime trees, a weak breeze wafted a strange sound toward the bed. You couldn't tell right away what kind of a sound it was: a child's crying, the song of Lazarus, or just wailing. You couldn't tell. But one thing was clear: the sound came from right below the window, and not from one throat but from many—there were trebles, altos, tenors.

"Barbara—they're cats!" Alyosha said. "My silly darling!"

"Cats? It can't be! What are those bass notes?"

"That's a sow grunting. Don't forget we're at a dacha here. Can't you hear? Yes, that's what it is, cats! Come on, calm down. Go back to sleep now."

Barbara and Alyosha lay down and pulled the blankets over their ears. The morning freshness had begun seeping through the window, and a slight chill hung in the air. Husband and wife curled up and closed their eyes. Five minutes later Alyosha turned round to the other side.

"They don't let you get any sleep, damn them! With all that screeching!"

In the meantime the feline song was reaching a crescendo. Powerful new voices were joining in, and what had started as a light rustle beneath the window gradually turned into a hubbub, then a rumpus, and finally a hullabaloo. What had begun as a sound tremulous as aspic jelly had finally reached a full fortissimo, and soon the air was full of ghastly notes. Some of the cats let out curt yelps, others rollicking trills—and exactly in rhythm, in octaves and alexandrines! Others sounded long sustained notes. One cat, it must have been the oldest and most passionate, sang in an unnatural voice, not a cat's voice, but at times in bass, at times in tenor.

"Meouw-meouw—tu tu tu—carrrrriou!"

If it hadn't been such a donnybrook, you would never think it was cats howling. Barbara turned over and muttered something. Alyosha jumped up, sent a few curses flying through the air, and closed the window. But windows are meager barriers: they let in sound, light, even electricity.

"I have to get up at eight to go to work," Alyosha shouted, "and these damn cats are howling! They won't let you sleep! Can't you at least shut up, woman? Whimpering like this in my ear! Whining at me like that! Is it my fault? They're not my cats!"

"Please, darling, chase them away!"

Her husband swore, jumped out of bed, and marched over to the window. Night was turning into morning.

Looking up at the sky, Alyosha saw only one little star. It

---

barely flickered in the mist. Sparrows chattered in the lime tree, startled by the sound of the opening window. Alyosha looked down into the garden and saw some ten cats. Their tails in the air, hissing and treading delicately on the grass, they howled, proceeding like a group of dromedaries around a pretty little cat who was sitting on an overturned washtub. It was hard to decide which was stronger: their love for the little cat or their self-importance. Had they come out of love, or just to show off? Their attitude betrayed the most refined scorn for each other. On the other side of the garden gate the sow with her piglets chafed against the grille, trying to get in.

"Shoo!" Alyosha hissed. "Shoo, you devils! Pshhh! Shoo!"

But the cats paid no attention. Only the cat in the middle looked in his direction, but even then casually, in passing. The cat was ecstatic; she didn't care about Alyosha.

"Shoo! Shoo! Damn you! Shoo, I wish you'd all go to hell! Barbara, give me that carafe there! I'll throw water on them! The devils!"

Barbara jumped out of bed and brought him not the carafe but a pitcher from the washstand. Alyosha leaned with his chest over the windowsill and tilted the pitcher out of the window.

"Gentlemen! Gentlemen!" he heard a voice above his head. "Young people nowadays! How can you do such a thing, huh? Ohhhhhh! The young people nowadays!"

A sigh followed. Alyosha looked up and saw a pair of shoulders in a calico dressing gown with a large flower pattern, and withered, sinewy fingers. From the shoulders protruded a small, gray-haired head with a nightcap, and the fingers were pointing down at him threateningly. The old man sat by the window without taking his eyes from the cats. His eyes were sparkling with longing, as if he were watching a ballet.

Alyosha's mouth fell open. He went white, and smiled.

"Are you resting well, Your Excellency?" he asked weakly.

"This is terrible! You are going against nature, young man! You could say, you are... hm, yes... actually sabotaging the laws of nature! This is terrible! How could you! These are... hm, yes... organisms. How do you say, yes, organisms! One must understand! Contemptible!"

Alyosha stepped back from the window, tiptoed to bed, and lay down meekly. Barbara curled up next to him and held her breath.

"That was our..." Alyosha whispered. "In person... he's not asleep. He loves cats. Damn! There's nothing worse than living with one's boss!"

"Young man!" Alyosha heard the old man's voice a minute later. "Where are you? Come out here please!"

Alyosha went to the window and looked up at the old man.

"Do you see that white cat there? What do you think of it? It's my cat! What carriage it has, what carriage! What a gait!

---

Just look at that! Meow, meow, Vaska! Vaska, darling! You naughty little thing, you! He's a pure Siberian. From far away... ha, ha, that little lady-cat over there—she'd better watch herself! My cat is always triumphant—you'll see what I mean! What carriage! What carriage!"

Alyosha replied that he found the animal's fur fabulous. The old man began talking about the life of the cat and all the things it did. Getting carried away, he spoke till sunrise, extolling every detail, smacking his lips and licking his sinewy fingers... so there was no going back to sleep.

The following night, at one in the morning, the cats again struck up their song, and again woke Barbara. Alyosha could not chase the cats away; His Excellency's cat was among them. Alyosha and Barbara listened to the cat concert till morning.

---

# HOW I CAME TO BE LAWFULLY WED

AFTER WE HAD FINISHED the punch, our parents murmured a few words to each other and left us alone.

"Go ahead!" my father whispered to me on his way out. "Say the words!"

"But how can I declare my love," I whispered back, "if I don't love her?"

"No one's asking what you want to do, you idiot!"

My father gave me an angry stare and left the garden pavilion. Then, after everyone had gone, a woman's hand reached in the half-open door and snatched the candle from the table. We sat in the dark.

"Well, there's no escaping now!" I thought, and with a dis-

---

reet cough I said briskly: "I see that circumstances favor me, Zoe Andreyevna! At last we are alone, and darkness comes to my aid, for it covers the shame written on my face... the shame pouring from the feelings with which my soul is ablaze."

Suddenly I stopped. I could hear Zoe Andreyevna's heart beating and her teeth chattering. Her whole organism was trembling—I could hear and feel it from the way the bench was shaking. The poor girl didn't love me. She hated me, the way a dog hates the stick that beats it. She despised me, you could say, as only an idiot can. Suddenly I feel like an orangutan, ugly—even though I'm covered in medals and honors—no better than a beast, fat-faced, pimply, covered with stubble; alcohol and a perpetual cold have made my nose red and bloated! A bear has more grace than I do. And don't even mention my intellectual qualities! With her, with Zoe, I had pulled an immoral trick before she became my bride. I stopped in mid-sentence, because suddenly I felt deeply sorry for her.

"Let us go out into the garden," I said. "It's stifling in here."

We went out and walked down the garden path. Our parents, who had been listening by the door, had managed to scamper into the bushes just before we appeared. The moonbeams played on Zoe's face. Idiot though I was, I thought I could read in that face all the sweet pain of bondage. I sighed and continued:

---

"The nightingale sings for its sweetheart... and I, all alone in this world, who can I sing to?"

Zoe blushed and lowered her eyes. She was acting to perfection the role she was expected to play. We sat on a bench by the stream, beyond which a church glimmered white. Behind the church towered Count Kuldarov's mansion, in which his clerk lived, Bolnitsin, the man Zoe loved. As she sat down on the bench she fixed her gaze on the mansion. My heart sank and shriveled with pity. My God, my God! May heaven smile on our parents... but they should be sent down to hell, for a week at least!

"All my happiness rests on a single person," I continued. "I feel deeply for that person... her perfume... I love her, and should she not return my love, then I am lost... dead... You are that person. Can you love me? Huh? Could you love me?"

"I love you," she whispered.

I must confess I almost died. I had thought she would dig in her heels, since she was deeply in love with someone else. I had relied on her passion for the other man, but things turned out quite differently. She wasn't strong enough to swim against the tide!

"I love you," she repeated, and burst into tears.

"But, no, that can't be!" I shouted, not knowing what I was saying, my whole body shaking. "How is it possible? Zoe Andreyevna—do not believe a word of what I said! My God, do not believe a word! May I roast in hell if I am in love with you! And you do not love me! This is all nonsense!"

I jumped up from the bench.

"We needn't go through with this! This is a farce! They are forcing us to marry for money, Zoe. What love is there between us? I would rather have a millstone around my neck than marry you! It's as simple as that! Damn! What right do they have to do this to us? What do they think we are? Serfs? Dogs? We won't get married! Damn them, the bastards! We've danced to their tune long enough already! I'm going to them right this minute to tell them that I won't marry you—it's as simple as that!"

Zoe suddenly stopped crying; her tears instantly dried up.

"I'm going to tell them right now!" I continued. "And you tell them too. Tell them that you don't love me—that it's Bolnitsin you love. And I'll be the first to shake Bolnitsin's hand... I'm fully aware of how deeply in love you are with him!"

Zoe smiled happily and came up to me.

"And you're in love with someone else too, aren't you?" she said, rubbing her hands together. "You're in love with Mademoiselle De Beux!"

"Yes," I said, "Mademoiselle De Beux. She's not Russian Orthodox, and she's not rich, but I love her for her mind and her edifying qualities. My parents can send me to hell, but I will marry her! I love her, I think I love her even more than I

---

love life itself! I cannot live without her! If I can't marry her, then I no longer wish to live! I'm going right this minute... let's both go and tell these fools... oh, thank you, my dearest...you have comforted me no end!"

My soul was flooded with happiness, and I thanked Zoe again and again, and she thanked me. And both of us, overjoyed, thankful, kissed each other's hands, commending each other on our high-mindedness. I kissed her hands; she kissed my forehead, the stubble of my beard. It seems that, forgetting all etiquette, I even hugged her! And let me tell you, this declaration of nonlove was sweeter than any declaration of love could be! Joyful, rosy, trembling all over, we rushed to the house to tell our parents of our decision. As we crossed the garden, we cheered each other on.

"So let them shout at us!" I said. "They can beat us, even throw us out, at least we'll be happy!"

We entered the house, and there, by the door, our parents were waiting. They took one look at us, saw how happy we were, and immediately called the butler. He brought in the champagne. I started protesting, waving my arms, stamping my feet.... Zoe began crying, shrieking...there was a tremendous uproar, a rumpus, and we didn't get to drink the champagne.

But they married us anyway.

Today is our silver wedding anniversary. We have lived together for a quarter of a century. Initially it was terrible. I swore at her, beat her, and then out of regret began loving her. This regret brought with it children... and then... well... we just got used to each other. This very moment my darling Zoe is standing right behind me. Laying her hands on my shoulders, she kisses my bald spot.

# FROM THE DIARY OF AN ASSISTANT BOOKKEEPER

MAY 11TH, 1863

Glotkin, our sixty-year-old bookkeeper, has been drinking milk laced with cognac for his cough, and as a result he has fallen into a violent alcoholic delirium. The doctors, with their typical self-confidence, confirm that he will die tomorrow. At last I will be bookkeeper! I have been promised this position for a long time now.

Kleshchev is to be tried for physically attacking an applicant who called him a bureaucrat. It seems that there will be a court case.

I had some fluid extracted from my stomach catarrh.

AUGUST 3RD, 1865

Glotkin, our bookkeeper, has a cold in his chest again. He is coughing and has started drinking milk laced with cognac. If he dies I will get his position. My hopes are high, but somewhat shaky—experience has shown that delirium tremens is not always fatal.

Kleshchev snatched a promissory note from an Armenian and tore it up. It seems that there will be a court case.

An old village woman (Guryevna) told me yesterday that what I have is not a catarrh, but a hidden hemorrhoid. It's quite possible!

### JUNE 30TH, 1867

The newspapers write that there's a cholera epidemic in Arabia. Maybe it will come to Russia, and there will be many job openings. Maybe the old bookkeeper will die and I will get his position. What vigor that man has! If you ask me, living such a long time is reprehensible.

I wonder what I should take for that catarrh of mine. Maybe some wormseed might do the trick.

### JANUARY 2ND, 1870

A dog was howling all night long in Glotkin's yard. Pelageya, my cook, says that this is a definite omen, and we stayed up until two in the morning talking about how once I become bookkeeper I will buy myself a raccoon coat and a dressing gown. And maybe I will even get married!

---

Obviously not to a young girl—I'm a bit too old for that—
but to a widow.

Yesterday Kleshchev was thrown out of the club for telling
a joke, at the top of his voice, mocking the patriotism of one
of the members of Ponyukhov's trade delegation. From what I
hear, Ponyukhov is taking him to court.

I think I'll go to Doctor Botkin for my catarrh. They say
he's good at healing....

### JULY 4TH, 1878

The newspapers report that the plague has hit Vetlyanka. People
are dropping like flies. As a precaution, Glotkin is drinking pepper vodka. As if pepper vodka would save an old fool like him!
If the plague hits here, I'll definitely be the new bookkeeper!

### JUNE 4TH, 1883

Glotkin is dying. I went to visit him, and crying bitter tears, I
begged forgiveness for having waited for his death with such
impatience. He forgave me magnanimously, and suggested I
drink acorn coffee for my catarrh.

Kleshchev again almost ended up in court: he rented a
piano and then pawned it to the Jews. And in spite of all this
he has a Stanislav medal and the rank of Collegiate Assessor.
It's amazing, the things that happen in this world!

Essence of Inbir—ten grams. Kalgan potion—seven

---

grams. Ostraya vodka—four grams. Seven-brother-blood—twenty grams. To cure catarrh, mix these with a liter of vodka and drink one wineglass of the mixture on an empty stomach.

### JUNE 7TH, 1883

Glotkin was buried yesterday. Alas! The old man's death was of no use to me! I see him in my dreams at night, wrapped in a shroud, beckoning. And woe unto me, the sinner—I did not become the bookkeeper, Chalikov did! It was not I who got the job, but a young man with the help of the general's wife's aunt! My hopes are dashed!

### JUNE 10TH, 1886

Chalikov's wife has run away. The poor man is distraught. Maybe grief will drive him to take his own life. If he does, I will be bookkeeper! There has already been talk. In other words, where there's life there's hope, and maybe the road to the raccoon coat will be short and sweet. As for getting married, it's not such a bad idea. Why not get married if the opportunity should arise? But I'll need some good advice—marriage is a serious step.

Kleshchev took Councillor Lirmanso's galoshes. It's a scandal!

Paysi the doorman suggested I use a mercuric chloride solution for my catarrh.

I'm going to try it.

———

# A FOOL; OR, THE RETIRED SEA CAPTAIN: A SCENE FROM AN UNWRITTEN VAUDEVILLE PLAY

*IT IS THE MARRIAGE season. Soufov is a retired sea captain. He is sitting on an oilskin sofa, with one leg resting over the other, his arms crossed. As he speaks he rocks back and forth. Lukinishna the matchmaker is a fat, sagging old woman sitting on a stool next to him. She has a foolish but good-natured face, with an expression of horror mixed with surprise. Seen from the side, she looks like a large snail; from the front, like a black beetle. She speaks servilely, and hiccups after every word.*

CAPTAIN: By the way, if you think about it, Ivan Nikolayevitch has set himself up quite nicely. He did well to get married. You can be a professor, a genius even, but if you're not married, you're not worth a brass kopeck! You've no census or public opinion worth mentioning. If you're not married, you don't carry any weight in society. Take me, for instance. I am a man from an educated background, a house owner, I have money, rank—even a medal! But what's the point? Who am I if you look at me from a point of view?—An old bachelor—a mere synonym, nothing more. (He pauses to think.) Everyone's married, everyone has children, except me—it's like in the song.... (He sings a few doleful lines in a deep baritone.) That's how my life is—surely there must be some woman left on the shelf for me to get married to!

LUKINISHNA: On the shelf? Lordy-lord, I'm sure we can do better than that! What with your noble nature, and... well, all your good qualities, and everything, we'll find you a woman—even one with money!

CAPTAIN: I don't need a woman with money. I wouldn't dream of doing such a despicable thing as marrying for money! I have my own money—I don't want to be eating from her plate, I want her to eat from mine! When you marry a poor woman, she's bound to feel and understand. I'm not that much of an egoist that I want to profit...

LUKINISHNA: Well, yes... and one thing's sure—a poor bride might well be prettier than a rich one...

———

CAPTAIN: But I'm not interested in looks either! What for? You can't use a pretty face as a cup and saucer! Beauty should not be in the flesh, it should be in the soul. What I need is goodness, meekness, you know, innocence... I want a wife who'll honor me, respect me...

LUKINISHNA: Yes! How can she not respect you if you're her lawfully wedded husband? It's not like she'd be uneducated or something!

CAPTAIN: Don't interrupt me! And I don't need an educated wife either! Nowadays, obviously, everyone's got an education, but there are different kinds of education. It's all well and good if your wife can prattle in French and German and God knows what else—it's very charming! But what use is all that if she can't, for instance, sew a simple button onto a shirt? I come from an educated background myself. I can show my face in any circle—I can sit down and chat with Prince Kanitelin as easily as I'm chatting with you right now, but I'm a simple man, and I need a simple girl. I'm not looking for intellect. In a man, intellect is important, but a female can get by quite nicely without much intellect.

LUKINISHNA: That's so very true! Even the newspapers are now saying that clever people are worthless!

---

CAPTAIN: A fool will both love you and respect you, and realize what my rank in life is. She will be fearful. A clever woman will eat your bread, but not feel whose bread she's eating. I want you to find me a fool! It's as simple as that! A fool! Do you have your eye on anyone?

LUKINISHNA: Oh, quite a few! (She thinks.) Let me see.... There are fools and there are fools... after all, even a foolish hen has her brainstorms! But you want a real idiot, right? (She thinks.) I know one, but I'm not sure if she's what you're looking for... she's from a merchant family and comes with a dowry of about five thousand... I wouldn't say she's downright ugly, she's, well, you know... neither here nor there. She's skinny, very thin... gentle, delicate... and she's kind, beyond the call of duty! She'd hand over her last piece of bread if you told her to! And she's meek—her mother could drag her through the house by the hair, and she wouldn't even squeak! And she fears her parents, she goes to church, and at home she's always ready to help! But when it comes to this... (She points to her forehead.) Do not judge me too harshly, sinful old woman that I am, for my plain-spokenness, for the forthright truth that I speak to you with the Lord as my witness: she's not all there up here! A complete fool! You can't get a word out of her, not a word, as if she were dead as a doornail. She'll sit there tight-lipped for hours, and suddenly, out of the blue—she'll jump up! As if you'd poured boiling water over her! She jumps up as if she were scalded and starts babbling... babbling, babbling... babbling endlessly... that her parents are fools, the food's awful, and all they do is lie, and that she has nowhere to go, that they ruined her life... "There's no way," the girl shouts, "that you can understand me!" The fool! A merchant called Kashalotov was wooing her—she turned him down! She laughed in his face! And he's rich, handsome, elegant, just like a young officer! And what does she do? She snatches up a stupid book, marches off to the pantry, and starts reading!

CAPTAIN: No she's not a fool of the right category... find me another! (He gets up and looks at his watch.) Well, bonjour for now. I'll be getting back to my bachelor business.

LUKINISHNA: Well, go right along! Go with God! (She gets up.) I'll drop by again Saturday evening with more about our bride.... (She walks over to the door.) And by the way, while you're getting back to your bachelor business, should I send you someone else for now?

# IN AUTUMN

NIGHT WAS ABOUT TO FALL. A crowd of coachmen and pilgrims was sitting in Uncle Tikhon's tavern. An autumn downpour with raging wet winds that lashed across their faces had driven them to seek refuge there. The tired, drenched travelers sat listening to the wind, dozing on benches by the wall. Boredom was written on their faces. One coachman, a pockmarked fellow with a scarred face, held a wet accordion on his knees: he played and stopped mechanically.

Outside the tavern door splashes of rain flew around the dim, grimy lantern. The wind howled like a wolf, yelping, as if to tear itself away from its tether by the door. From the yard came the sound of horses snorting and hoofs thudding in the mud. It was dank and cold.

---

Uncle Tikhon, a tall peasant with a fat face and small, drowsy, deep-set eyes, sat behind the counter. In front of him on the other side of the counter stood a man of about forty, in clothes that were dirty and shabby but respectable. He was wearing a wrinkled summer coat covered with mud, calico pants, and rubber galoshes without shoes. His head, his thin pointed elbows, and the hands jammed into his pockets were shivering feverishly. From time to time a sudden spasm ran down his whole gaunt body, from his horribly haggard face to his rubber galoshes.

"For Christ's sake!" he said to Tikhon in his scratchy, broken bass. "Give me a drink... just a little one, that glass there! You can put it on my tab!"

"You bet I can! Nothing but scoundrels in here!"

The scoundrel looked at Tikhon with contempt, with hatred. If he could, he would have murdered him then and there.

"You just don't understand, you lout, you numskull! It's not me begging—from deep within my guts—as you say in your peasant lingo! It's my illness begging! Can't you see that?"

"There's nothing to see! Get out!"

"You must understand! If I don't get a drink now, if I don't assuage my passion, I'm quite capable of committing a crime! By God, I'm quite capable! You bastard, you've been handing out drinks to drunkards for ages in your damn tavern! And you're telling me that till today you never gave a thought to what they were? Sick people, that's what! You can chain them up, beat them, flail them—as long as you give them their vodka! I humbly beg you! I implore you! I'm demeaning myself.... Lord, how I am demeaning myself!" The scoundrel shook his head and spat on the floor.

"Give me money, and you'll have your vodka!" Tikhon said.

"Where am I supposed to get money from? I've drunk it all! This coat's all I've got left. I can't give it to you, I'm not wearing anything underneath... d'you want my hat?"

The scoundrel gave Tikhon his felt hat, whose lining was showing through here and there. Tikhon took the hat, looked at it, and shook his head.

"I wouldn't take this if you gave it to me for nothing!" he said. "It's a piece of shit!"

"You don't like it? Then give me a drink on credit if you don't like it. When I come back from town I'll give you your fiver! Then you can choke on it! Yes, choke on it!"

"You trying to con me? What kind of a man are you? What did you come here for?

"I want a drink. Not me, my illness! Do you understand?"

"Why are you bothering me? The road outside is full of scum like you! Go ask them in the name of Christ to give you

———

a drink. All I'll hand out in the name of Christ is bread! You swine!"

"You can fleece them, the poor bastards, but me—I'm sorry, I can't take their money! Not me!"

The scoundrel suddenly stopped, blushed, and turned to the pilgrims.

"That's an idea! You're Christians! Will you sacrifice a fiver? I beg you from deep within my guts! I'm ill!"

"Drink water!" the small man with the pock-marked face laughed.

The scoundrel felt ashamed. He started coughing heavily and then fell silent. A few moments later he started pleading again with Tikhon. Finally he burst into tears and began offering his wet coat for a glass of vodka. In the darkness no one could see his tears, and no one took his coat because among the pilgrims there were women who did not want to see a man's nakedness.

"What am I to do now?" the scoundrel asked in a quiet voice full of despair. "What am I to do? I have to have a drink, or I might well commit a crime... even resort to suicide... what am I going to do?"

He began pacing up and down.

The mail coach rolled up, its bells ringing. The wet postman came in, drank a glass of vodka, and left. The mail coach drove on.

---

"I have something golden I'll give you," the scoundrel, suddenly deathly pale, said to Tikhon. "Yes, I'll give it to you. So be it! Even if what I'm doing is low-down, vile—here, take it... I am doing this despicable deed because I'm beside myself... even if I was brought before a court of law, I would be forgiven. Take it, but only on one condition: that you give it back to me when I return. I'm giving it to you before witnesses!"

The scoundrel slid his wet hand inside his coat and took out a small gold medallion. He opened it and glanced at the portrait inside.

"I should take the portrait out, but I have nowhere to put it—I'm soaked. Damn you, take it with the portrait. But on one condition... my dear fellow... I beg you... don't touch this face with your fingers. I beg you, my dear fellow! Forgive me for having been so rude to you, for saying the things I said... I'm an idiot... just don't touch it with your fingers, and don't look at the face!"

Tikhon took the medallion, inspected it, and put it in his pocket.

"Stolen goods," he said, and filled a glass. "Well, fine! Drink!"

The drunkard took the glass in his hand. His eyes flashed, as much as his strength allowed his drunken, bleary eyes to flash, and he drank, drank with feeling, with convulsive pauses. Having drunk away the medallion with the portrait, he lowered his eyes with shame and went to a corner. There he perched on a bench next to the pilgrims, curled up, and closed his eyes.

Half an hour passed in stillness and silence. Only the wind howled, blowing its autumn rhapsody over the chimney. The women pilgrims were praying and soundlessly settling under the benches for the night. Tikhon opened the medallion and looked at the woman's face smiling out of the golden frame, at the tavern, at Tikhon, at the bottles.

A wagon creaked outside. There was a rattling sound and then the thudding of boots in the mud. A short peasant with a pointed beard came running in. He was wet, wearing a long sheepskin coat covered in mud.

"There you go!" he shouted, banging a fiver down on the counter. "A glass of Madeira! Make it a good one!"

And rakishly swiveling around on one foot, he ran his eye over the people in the tavern. "Made of sugar, are you? Chicken feathers upon thine aunt! Scared of the rain? Ha! Poor things! Who's this raisin here?"

He went over to the scoundrel and looked him in the face.

"Oh! Your lordship!" he said. "Semyon Sergeyitch! Good heavens! What? How come you're hanging about here in this tavern in such a state? What are you doing here? Suffering martyr!"

---

The squire looked at the peasant and covered his face with his sleeve. The peasant sighed, shook his head, waved his hands about in despair, and went to the counter to finish his drink.

"That's our master," he whispered to Tikhon, nodding toward the scoundrel. "Our landowner, Semyon Sergeyitch. Look at him! Look what he looks like now! Ha! Just look at that! What drink can do to you!"

The peasant gulped down his drink, wiped his mouth with his sleeve, and continued: "I'm from his village. Four hundred versts from here, from Akhtilovka... my folks were his father's serfs! Sad, ain't it! His lordship was such a splendid gentleman. This horse here, the one outside, you see it? He gave it me! Ha! That's fate for you!"

The coachmen and pilgrims started crowding round the peasant. In a quiet voice, over the noises of autumn, he told them the story. Semyon Sergeyitch remained sitting in the same corner, his eyes closed, muttering to himself. He was listening too.

"It happened because of weakness," the peasant said, gesticulating with his hands. "Too much good life! He was a rich gentleman—powerful, in the whole province! Eat, drink, cart-loads! How many times he drove past this very tavern in his carriage—you must have seen him! He was rich! Five years ago he was going through Mikishkinski on a barge, and instead of a

fiver he gave the man a whole ruble! His ruin was so stupid.
Mainly because of a woman. He fell in love, head over heels,
with a woman from town—he loved her more than his life. But
he didn't fall in love with a shining falcon. She was a black crow.
Marya Egorovna, that was that damn woman's name, and with
a strange last name too—you can't even pronounce it. He loved
her and proposed to her, all God-fearing and correct. Then, they
say, she said yes. After all, his lordship wasn't just anybody—he
was sober and rolling in money.... Then one evening, I remember well, I'm walking through the garden. I look, and there they
are sitting on the bench kissing. He gives her one kiss, and she,
the viper, gives him two back! He kisses her hand, and her, she
blushes. Then she squeezes herself close to him, damn her! I love
you, she says, Semyon... and Semyon goes about as if bewitched,
boasting of his happiness like a fool... handing out a ruble here,
two there, and me he gave this horse outside! He was so happy,
he dropped everyone's debts! Then came the wedding. They got
married all nice and proper. Then, as everyone's at the dinner,
she gets up and goes with the carriage into town to the attorney,
who's her lover. Right after the wedding, the harlot! At the high
point! Ha! Then he went nuts, started drinking! Look at him!
He's running around like a half-wit thinking of nothing but that
harlot! He loves her! I bet he's on his way to town just so he can
get a glimpse of her... But the other thing, let me tell you, the
thing that really ruined him, was his brother-in-law—his sister's

———————

husband. The squire took it into his head to guarantee his brother-in-law with the bank—around thirty thousand he guaranteed! They say the scoundrel of a brother-in-law knows how to squeeze a stone—he just sat back and waited, and our master had to pay the whole thirty thousand! A fool suffers for his foolishness! His wife had children with her attorney, his brother-in-law bought an estate near Poltava, and our master wanders around from one tavern to the next like a fool, making us all listen to his moaning: "Lost have I, dear brothers, my faith in mankind! There is no one I can, how shall I put it, believe in!" Weakness, that's what it is! We all have problems! So what are we supposed to do—start drinking? There's this corporal we used to have in the army. His wife brings the schoolmaster to her house in broad daylight—she spends all her husband's money on drink. And that corporal walks about grinning. The only effect was he lost some weight!"

"The Lord does not provide everyone with that kind of strength!" Tikhon said.

"Yeah, everyone's strength is different, that's true!"

The peasant spoke for a long time. When he finished, the tavern was silent.

"Hey, you... how're you feeling? You unlucky man! Here, drink!" Tikhon said, turning to the squire.

The squire came up to the counter and drank the vodka with delight.

---

"Give me the medallion for a second!" he whispered to Tikhon. "Just one look and… I'll give it back to you!"

Tikhon frowned, and without saying a word handed him the medallion. The fellow with the pockmarked face sighed, shook his head, and asked for a vodka.

"Have a drink, your lordship! Hmm! Life is good without vodka, but it's even better with it! With vodka even sorrow's not sorrow! Drink up!"

After five glasses the squire sat down in his corner, opened the medallion, and with clouded, drunken eyes looked for the beloved face. But the face was gone. It had fallen out of the medallion when Tikhon opened it.

The lantern flared up and went out. In the corner a woman pilgrim was mumbling in delirium. The fellow with the pockmarked face prayed aloud and then lay down on the bench. Another traveler came in. The rain poured and poured. It got colder and colder, and it seemed as if there would be no end to this vile, dark autumn. The squire was still staring at the medallion, looking for the woman's face. The candle went out.

Spring, where are you?

# THE GRATEFUL GERMAN

I ONCE KNEW A GRATEFUL GERMAN. The first time I met him was in Frankfurt-am-Main. He was walking along Dummstrasse with a monkey on a leash. One could read on the German's face hunger, love of the fatherland, and resignation. He sang a plaintive song, and the monkey danced. I took pity on them and gave them a coin.

"Thank you!" the German said to me, pressing it to his heart. "I shall remember your kindness to my dying day!"

The second time I met the German was in Frankfurt-an-der-Oder. He was walking along the Eselstrasse selling fried sausages. The moment he saw me tears ran down his cheeks, and he lifted his eyes to heaven.

"I thank you, mein Herr!" he said. "I will never forget the

coin with which you saved both me and my late monkey from starving! Your coin gave us comfort!"

The third time I met him was here in Russia. He was teaching Russian children ancient languages, trigonometry, and musical theory. In his free time, after classes, he was trying to get a job as a railroad inspector.

"Ah, I remember you!" he said to me, shaking my hand. "All Russians are bad people, except for you. I can't stand the Russians, but I shall remember that coin you gave me to my dying day!"

We never met again.

# A SIGN OF THE TIMES

THEY DECLARED THEIR LOVE in a drawing room with light blue wallpaper.

The young man of pleasant appearance knelt before the young woman and vowed his love.

"I can not live without you, my dearest!" he sighed. "I swear, the moment I set eyes on you I was lost! Dearest, tell me... tell me... yes or no?"

The girl opened her mouth to answer, but at that moment her brother's head appeared at the door.

"Lily, can you come here a minute?" her brother asked.

"What is it?" Lily replied, and followed him out of the room.

"I'm sorry to disturb you, but I am your brother, and it's

---

my sacred duty to caution you... Be careful with that man. Say as little as possible—only what you have to."

"But he's proposing!"

"That's fine! Declare your love, marry him, but for God's sake be careful! I know what I'm talking about—he's a complete scoundrel! Give him half a chance, and he'll sell us out!"

"Oh, Max, thank you! I had no idea!"

The young woman went back into the living room, answered the young man with a yes, kissed him, let him embrace her, and vowed she would be his. But she stepped carefully—she spoke only of love.

———

# FROM THE DIARY OF A YOUNG GIRL

OCTOBER 13TH
Finally something is happening on my street too! I look out and can't believe my eyes. A tall, stately, brown-haired man with dark, fiery eyes is pacing up and down beneath my window. His mustache—exquisite! He's been pacing there for five days now, from early morning till late at night, and he's constantly looking up at our windows! I pretend not to notice.

OCTOBER 15TH
It's been pouring rain since early this morning, and the poor man is still walking up and down. As a reward I made eyes at him and blew him a kiss. He answered with the most charm-

---

ing smile. Who is he? My sister Varya says he's in love with her, and that it's because of her that he's out there in the rain. She's so naive! Is a dark-haired man likely to fall in love with a dark-haired girl? Mama sent us to put on something more elegant and sit by the window. "He might be a swindler or something, but he could well be a respectable gentleman," she said. A swindler! Quel... Mummy, you are so silly!

## OCTOBER 16TH

Varya says I've ruined her life. As if it were my fault that he loves me and not her! I unintentionally dropped a note onto the sidewalk. The naughty man—he wrote "later" with chalk on his sleeve! Then he walked up and down, and wrote on the gate across the way: "Yes, let's meet! Later!" He wrote it in chalk, and then quickly erased it. Oh, why does my heart beat thus?

## OCTOBER 17TH

Varya hit me in the chest with her elbow, the mean, despicable, jealous beast! Today he stopped a policeman and spoke to him for a long time about something or other, pointing up at our windows. The plot thickens! He must be bribing him... O men, you are such tyrants and despots, and yet how cunning and wonderful you are!

---

OCTOBER 18TH

After a long absence, my brother Sergei came back tonight. He didn't even have time to lie down before they summoned him to the police station.

OCTOBER 19TH

The vermin! The beast! It turns out that for the past twelve days he's been trying to catch my brother Sergei, who seems to have embezzled some money.

Today he wrote on the gate: "I'm free now, we can meet." The swine! I stuck my tongue out at him!

---

# THE STATION-MASTER

THE STATIONMASTER AT Drebesky is called Stephan Stephanitch—his family name is Sheptunov. Last summer he was involved in a minor scandal. Insignificant though it was, this scandal cost him a great deal. Because of it he lost his new stationmaster's cap and his trust in humanity.

In the summer, train number 8 would pass his station at 2:40 in the morning, the most inconvenient time possible. Instead of sleeping, Stephan Stephanitch had to walk up and down the platform and stick around the telegraph office until morning.

Every summer Aleutov, his assistant, would leave to get married, and poor Sheptunov had to hold the fort on his own.

---

Fate had dealt him a harsh blow! But not every evening was boring. Sometimes Marya Ilinishna, the bailiff Kutsapyetov's wife, would come over from the neighboring estate and visit him at the station. She was not particularly young, or particularly beautiful, but gentlemen, let's face it: at night you can mistake a pillar for a policeman, or as the saying goes, "Boredom, like hunger, doth not a bosom buddy make." So anything will do. When Madam Kutsapyetov came to the station, Sheptunov would take her by the arm, climb down the platform, and head for the freight cars. There by the cars, waiting for train number 8, he would begin declaiming vows, and keep it up right to the moment the train whistle blew.

One fine night he was standing by the cars with Marya Ilinishna, waiting for the train. The cloudless sky was quiet, and the moon shimmered gently, casting its rays on the station, the field, the boundless expanse. All around them was quiet, serene. Sheptunov held his arm around Marya's waist and was silent. She too was silent. Both stood in some kind of sweet light, quiet like the moon, forgotten.

"What fabulous weather!" Sheptunov would sigh from time to time. "You're not cold, are you?"

Instead of answering, she would snuggle up closer and closer to his uniform.

At 2:20 in the morning the stationmaster looked at the clock and said, "The train will be coming any minute. Come

---

on, Marya, let's gaze at the tracks: whoever sees the train lights first will be the one whose love is stronger... let's watch."

They stared into the wide expanse. Here and there faint lights shone softly along the endless tracks. The train was not yet to be seen. Looking off into the distance, Sheptunov saw something strange. He saw two long shadows striding over the rails. The shadows were moving right toward him, becoming bigger and wider.... One of the figures seemed to emanate from a person's body, the second from a long stick, which the figure was holding.

The shadow was coming closer. It was whistling an aria from Madam Ango.

"Do not walk on the rails! It is forbidden!" Sheptunov shouted. "Get off the tracks!"

"Don't order me about, you swine!" the answer came back.

Outraged, Sheptunov rushed forward, but Marya Ilinishna grabbed his coattail.

"For God's sake, Stepa!" she whispered. "It's my husband! Nazark!"

She had barely uttered the words when Kutsapyetov appeared in front of the stunned stationmaster. The stunned stationmaster cried out, banged his head against something metallic, and dove under a car. He wiggled out from under it on his belly and ran along the right-of-way. Jumping across the ties, stumbling over the rails, he ran toward the water tower like a dog with a tin can tied to its tail.

"That stick... that stick he's carrying!" he thought as he bolted.

At the water tower he stopped to catch his breath, but he heard footsteps behind him. He looked back and saw the fast-moving shadow of a man with the shadow of a stick. Panic-stricken, he ran on.

"Wait a minute! Stop!" he heard Kutsapyetov's voice behind him. "Stop! Watch out! The train!"

Sheptunov looked forward and saw the train with its ter-rifying, fiery eyes. His hair stood on end. His pounding heart suddenly froze. Gathering all his strength, he jumped into the darkness. For about four seconds he flew through the air, and then fell on something hard and slanted and began rolling down, snatching at burdocks.

"I'm on the embankment!" he thought. "Well, it doesn't matter. Better a safe fool rolling down an embankment than a nobleman beaten black and blue by a lout!"

A large, heavy boot stepped into a puddle by his right ear. He felt two hands prodding his back.

"Is that you?" he heard Kutsapyetov's voice. "Is that you, Stephan Stephanitch?"

"Have mercy!" Sheptunov moaned.

"What's wrong with you, my dear fellow? What is it that

---

frightened you? It's me, Kutsapyetov! Don't tell me you didn't recognize me! I ran after you as fast as I could. I even called out! My dear fellow, that train almost ran over you! When Marya saw you run like that, she too was seized with fright, and fainted on the platform. Maybe my calling you a swine frightened you! Please don't be offended! I thought you were a railroad worker!"

"Do not mock me! If you are here for vengeance, go ahead! I am in your hands!" Sheptunov moaned. "Beat me, maim me!"

"My dear fellow, what's wrong with you? I came here to talk about something. I ran after you to talk business!"

Kutsapyetov was silent for a few seconds, and then continued: "It's an important matter. My Marya told me that you like a bit of hanky-panky with her. As far as that goes, it's fine by me. You see, when it comes to these matters I personally don't give a damn, but if we look at the situation fair and square, I would be honored if you would be ready to come to some sort of an accomodation with me. After all, I am her husband, the head of the family, you might say... legally speaking. When Prince Mikhail Dimitritch was hanky-pankying with her, he would slip me two twenty-fivers a month. How much would you settle for? An honest man's word is good as gold. But please, get up!"

Sheptunov stood up. Broken, sullied, he dragged himself up the embankment.

"How much would you settle for?" Kutsapyetov repeated.

———

"I was thinking of only asking for a twenty-fiver... because I wanted to see if you might have a little position available for my nephew."

In a daze, Sheptunov stumbled blindly to the station and threw himself on the bed. When he woke up the next morning, his cap and one of his shoulder straps were missing.

To this day he is ashamed.

# A WOMAN'S REVENGE

THE BELL RANG.

Nadyezhda Petrovna, the lady of the house in which this story took place, jumped up from the sofa and ran to open the door.

"It'll be my husband!" she thought.

But when she opened the door, it wasn't her husband she saw. A tall, handsome man in an expensive bear-fur coat and gold-rimmed spectacles stood before her. There was a frown on his forehead, and his sleepy eyes looked out on the world with languid indifference.

"How may I help you?" Nadyezhda Petrovna asked.

"I am the doctor, madam. I was called here by... let me see, the Chelobitevs. Do the Chelobitevs live here?"

"Yes, we are the Chelobitevs. But... I'm sorry, doctor. My

husband had an abscess on his gum and a fever. He sent you a letter, but as it looked like you weren't coming, he lost patience and rushed off to the dentist's."

"I see. But he might as well have gone straight to the dentist without inconveniencing me."

The doctor frowned. A minute passed in silence.

"I am sorry, doctor, that we inconvenienced you, that we had you come all this way for nothing. If my husband had known that you were coming, I can assure you he would never have run off to the dentist's! I am so sorry!"

Another minute of silence passed. Nadyezhda Petrovna scratched her head.

"What is he waiting for?" she thought, glancing at the door.

"I have to go, madam!" the doctor mumbled. "Please don't keep me. Time is money!"

"Well... I, well... I'm not keeping you."

"But madam! I cannot leave without being compensated for my efforts!"

"Your efforts?... Oh, I see!" Nadyezhda Petrovna stammered, turning bright red. "You are right... it's true, you must be paid for coming... you went to all that trouble, you came over! But doctor, this is very embarrassing... my husband left home taking all our money with him! I don't have a kopeck in the house!"

"Well... that's strange. Let me see. I can't wait for your

husband to return, but if you look carefully through the house you might find a little money... the amount, in actual fact, would be quite negligible."

"But I can assure you, my husband took everything with him! I am sorry, this is so embarrassing! I would never want to go through all of this for a few rubles... what an impossible situation!"

"I have never understood the public's view of a doctor's job, never! It's as if we ourselves weren't people, as if our job wasn't a job! After all, I did come over to your house, I lost time, I was inconvenienced!"

"No, I'm fully aware of what you're saying, but you will surely agree that there are times when there isn't even a kopeck in the house!"

"That may well be. But what it is, is that you, madam, are simply... naïve, illogical. You must understand, not paying a person... that's unethical. You take advantage of the fact that I can't take you to court, and so... simply and without ceremony... it's so strange!"

The doctor fell silent. He was disgusted with humanity. Nadyezhda Petrovna blushed. She felt awkward.

"Fine!" she said sharply. "Wait for me here, and I'll send word to the store to see if I can borrow some money. I'll pay you."

Nadyezhda Petrovna went into the living room and sat

---

down to write a note to the storekeeper. The doctor took off his coat, went into the living room, and slumped down on a chair. They both sat silently, waiting for a response from the storekeeper. About five minutes later the answer came. Nadyezhda Petrovna took a ruble out of the envelope and gave it to the doctor. The doctor's eyes bulged.

"Surely you are joking, madam!" he said, laying the ruble on the table. "My manservant might accept a ruble, but I... no, I'm sorry!"

"But how much would you need?"

"Normally I would take ten. From you, however, five would be fine."

"You'll have to wait quite a long time before you'll get a fiver from me! I don't have the money."

"Send another note to the storekeeper. If he could give you a ruble, why shouldn't he be able to give you five? Does it matter? I beg you, madam, not to keep me any longer! I am a busy man!"

"Doctor, you are being unkind! You are being impertinent... rude... inhuman! You are... loathsome!"

Nadyezhda Petrovna turned to the window and bit her lip. Big tears fell from her eyes.

"Scoundrel! Bastard!" she thought. "Animal! How dare he, how dare he! Can't he understand my horrible, impossible situation! Just you wait, you swine!"

———

After a few seconds of thought, she turned to face the doctor. This time her face expressed suffering.

"Doctor!" she said in a low, imploring voice. "Doctor! If you had a heart, if you tried to understand, you wouldn't torture me this way for the money. As it is, my life is full of trials and tribulations!"

Nadyezhda Petrovna squeezed her temples as if she were squeezing a spring. Her hair spilled onto her shoulders.

"One suffers as it is being married to a lout of a husband... one is forced to bear these horrendous surroundings, and then on top of it all one is reproached by the only educated person around! My God! I can't bear it any longer!"

"But madam, please understand, the special conditions of our profession..."

But the doctor was forced to cut his sentence short. Nadyezhda Petrovna staggered and fainted into his outstretched arms. Her head fell onto his shoulder.

"Here, near the fireplace, yes," she whispered after a few moments. "Come closer... I will tell you everything... everything!"

An hour later the doctor left the Chelobitev apartment. He felt annoyed, ashamed, and happy all in one.

"Damn it!" he thought, as he sat down in his sleigh. "It's never a good idea to take too much money with you when you leave the house. You never know what you'll run up against!"

———

# O WOMEN, WOMEN!

SERGEI KUZMITCH Pochitayev, editor-in-chief of the provincial newspaper *Flypaper*, came home from the office tired and worn out, and slumped down on the sofa.

"Thank God I'm finally home! Here I can rest my soul... by our warm hearth, with my wife, my darling, the only person in this world who understands me, who can truly sympathize with me!"

"Why are you so pale today?" his wife, Marya Denisovna, asked.

"My soul was in torment, but now—the moment I'm with you, I'm fully relaxed!"

"What happened?"

"So many problems, especially today! Petrov is no longer willing to extend credit to the paper. The secretary has taken to drink... I can somehow deal with all these things, but here's the real problem, Marya. There I am, sitting in my office going over something one of my reporters wrote, when suddenly the door opens and my dear old friend Prince Prochukhantsev comes in. You know, the one who always plays the beau in amateur theatricals—he's the one who gave his white horse to that actress, Zryakina, for a single kiss. The moment I saw him I thought: what the hell brings him here, he must want something! But I reckoned he'd probably come to promote Zryakina. So we start chatting about this and that. Finally it turns out that he hadn't come to push Zryakina—he brought some poems for me to print! 'I felt,' he tells me, 'a fiery flame and... a flaming fire! I wanted to taste the sweetness of authorship!'

"So he takes a perfumed pink piece of paper out of his pocket and hands it to me.

"'In my verse,' he continues, 'I am, in actual fact, somewhat subjective, but anyway... after all, our national poet Nekrassov was deeply subjective, too.'

"I picked up these subjective poems and read them through. It was the most impossible drivel I have ever seen! Reading these poems, you feel your eyes beginning to pop and your stomach about to burst, as if you'd swallowed a millstone!

———

And he dedicated the poems to Zryakina! I would drag him to court if he dared dedicate such drivel to me! In one poem he uses the word 'headlong' five times! And the rhythm! 'Lilee-white' instead of 'lily-white!' He rhymes 'horse' with 'of course!'

"'I'm sorry!' I tell him, 'You are a very dear friend, but there is no way I can print your poems!'

"'And why, may I ask?'

"'Because... well, for reasons beyond the control of the editorial office, these poems do not fit into the scheme of the newspaper.'

"I went completely red. I started rubbing my eyes, and claimed I had a pounding headache. How could I tell him that his poems were utterly worthless! He saw my embarrassment, and puffed up like a turkey.

"'You,' he tells me, 'are angry with Zryakina, and that's why you're refusing to print my poems! I understand! I fully understand, my dear sir!'

"He accused me of prejudice, called me a Philistine, an ecclesiastical bigot, and God knows what else. He went at me for a full two hours. In the end he swore he would get even with me. Then he left without saying another word. That's the long and short of it, darling! And today's the fourth of December, no less—Saint Barbara's day—Zryakina's name day! He wanted those poems printed, come wind, come rain! As far as printing them goes, that's impossible! My paper would become a laughingstock throughout Russia. But not to print them is impossible too: Prochukhantsev will start plotting against me—and that'll be that! I have to figure out now how to get myself out of this impossible mess!"

"What kind of poems are they? What are they about?" Marya Denisovna asked.

"They're useless, pure twaddle! Do you want to hear one? It starts like this:

*Through dreamily wafting cigar smoke,*
*You came scampering into my dreams,*
*Your love hitting me with one sharp stroke,*
*Your sweet lips smiling with fiery beams.*

"And then straightaway:

*Forgive me, O angel pure as a summer song!*
*Eternal friend, O ideal so very bright!*
*Forgetting love, I threw myself headlong*
*Into the jaws of death—O woe, O fright!*

"And on and on. Pure twaddle!"

"What do you mean? These poems are really sweet!" Marya Denisovna exclaimed, clasping her hands together.

"They are extremely sweet! You're just being churlish,

Sergei!... 'Through dreamily wafting cigar smoke... sweet lips smiling with fiery beams,' you simply don't understand, do you? You don't!"

"It is you who don't understand, not I!"

"No, I'm sorry! I may be at sea when it comes to prose, but when it comes to poetry, I'm in my element! You just hate him, and that's why you don't want to print his poems!"

The editor sighed and banged his hand first on the table, and then against his forehead.

"Experts!" he muttered, smiling scornfully.

Snatching up his top hat, he shook his head bitterly and went out.

"I will go look for a corner of this world where a shunned man can find some sympathy! O women, women! They are all the same!" he thought, as he marched over to the London Restaurant. He intended to get himself drunk.

———

# TWO LETTERS

## I. A SERIOUS QUESTION

My dearest uncle Anisim Petrovitch,

Your neighbor Kurosheyev has just been to visit me and informed me, among other things, that Murdashevitch, from next door to you, returned with his family from abroad a few days ago. This bit of news shocked me all the more as it seemed that the Murdashevitches were going to stay abroad forever. My dearest uncle! If you harbor any love in your heart for your humble nephew, then I beg you, dear, dear uncle, to visit Murdashevitch and find out how his ward, Mashenka, is doing. I am laying bare to you the innermost secret of my soul. It is only you alone I trust! I love Mashenka—I love her passionately, more than my life! Six years of separation have not dampened my feelings for her one iota. Is she alive? Is she well? Please write and tell me how she is! Does she remember me? Does she love me like she used to? May I write her a letter? My dear, dear uncle! Please find out and send me all the details.

Tell her that I am no longer the poor and timid student she once knew—I am now a barrister, with a practice of my own, with money. In a word, to achieve perfect happiness in life I need only one thing—her!

I embrace you, and hope for a speedy reply.

Vladimir Gretchnev

## II. A Detailed Response

My dearest nephew Vladimir,

I received your letter, and went over to see Murdashevitch the very next day. What a great fellow he is! He did age a bit abroad, and has gone somewhat gray, but all these years he kept me, his dear old friend, in his heart, and when I entered he embraced me, looked me in the eye for a long time, and said with a timid, tender cry, "Who are you?" When I told him my family name, he embraced me again, and said, "Now it's all coming back to me!" What a great fellow! As long as I was there, I had a few drinks and a snack, and then we sat down to a few friendly rounds of Preference. He explained to me all kinds of funny things about foreign countries and had me in stitches with all his droll imitations of the Germans and their funny ways. But in science, he told me, the Germans have gone far. He even showed me a picture he bought on his trip through Italy, of this person of the female sex in a rather strange, indecent dress. And I saw Mashenka too. She was wearing a plush pink-colored gown embellished with all kinds of costly bits and bobs. She does remember you, and her eyes even cried a tear or two when she asked about you. She wants you to write to her, and thanks you for your tender memories and feelings. You wrote that you have your own practice and money! My dear boy, do be careful with that money—be moderate and abstinent! When I was a young man I gave myself up to voluptuous excesses—but only for short periods, and with extreme caution—and yet I still repent!

My very best wishes.

Your loving uncle, Anisim Gretchnev

P.S. Your writing is garbled, but has an eloquent and tempting style. I showed your letter to all the neighbors. They thought you a great storyteller! Vladimir, Father Grigory's son, copied it out so he can send it to a newspaper. I also showed it to Mashenka and her husband, Uhrmacher, the German she

---

married last year. He read it and was full of praise. I am going to show the letter and read it to others, too. You must write more! Murdashevitch's caviar is very tasty.

———

# TO SPEAK OR BE SILENT: A TALE

ONCE UPON A TIME in a distant kingdom there lived two friends, Krueger and Smirnov. Krueger had a brilliant mind; Smirnov, on the other hand, was not so clever: he was unassuming, meek, and weak-willed. Krueger was talkative and eloquent, Smirnov tight-lipped.

One day, while traveling on a train, both men tried to win the affections of a young woman in the compartment. Krueger took the seat next to her and ingratiated himself with her, while Smirnov sat silently, blinking, lustfully licking his lips. At the next station Krueger got off with the young woman and didn't return for quite a while. When he came back, he winked at Smirnov and clicked his tongue.

"You're so smooth!" Smirnov said to him, full of envy.

"How do you do it? You hardly sat down next to her, and

that was that... Lucky you!"

"You keep letting opportunities slip through your fingers! You sat right next to her for three hours, and not a word! Silent as a log! In our world, my friend, silence brings you nothing. You have to be quick on the draw, talkative. Nothing works for you—and why? Because you're a milksop!"

Smirnov agreed with these arguments, and decided deep in his heart to change his ways. Within the hour, overcoming his timidity, he was sitting next to a gentleman in a blue suit and striking up a lively conversation with him. The gentleman turned out to be extremely talkative and immediately began asking Smirnov all kinds of questions, principally of a scientific nature. He asked him how he liked the land, the sky, was he satisfied with the laws of nature and with society, touching on European trends of free thinking, the status of women in America, and so on. Smirnov answered with wit and enthusiasm.

Imagine how surprised he was when the gentleman in the blue suit grabbed him by the arm at the next station and, smiling spitefully, barked out: "Follow me!"

Smirnov followed him and disappeared. No one knew where he was. Two years later, pale, emaciated, scraggy, like the skeleton of a fish, he ran into Krueger. Smirnov smiled bitterly and told him all the hardships he had been through.

"You mustn't be an idiot and blab so much!" Krueger said. "You have to know when to hold your tongue!"

———

# AFTER THE FAIR

A MERCHANT FROM THE First Traders Guild of Moscow had just returned from the Nizhgorod Fair, and in his pockets his wife found a bunch of torn and tattered papers covered with smudged writing. She managed to make out the following:

Dear Mr. Semyon Ivanovitch:

Mr. Khryapunov, the artiste you beat up, is prepared to reach an out-of-court settlement of 100 rubles. He will not accept one kopeck less. I await your answer.

Sincerely, your lawyer, N. Erzayev.

To the brute who dares call himself a trader:

Having been insulted by you most grossly, I have relegated my complaint to a court of law. As you seem incapable of appreciating who I am, perhaps the justice of the peace or a public trial will teach you to respect me. Erzayev, your lawyer, said that you were not prepared to pay me a hundred rubles. This being the case, I am prepared to accept 75 rubles in compensation for your brutish behavior. It is only in lenience for your simplemindedness and to what one could call your animalistic instincts that I am prepared to let you off so cheaply. When an educated man insults me, I charge much more.

Khryapunov, artiste

...concerning our demand of 539 rubles and 43 kopecks, the value of the broken mirror and the piano you demolished in the Glukharev Restaurant...

...anoint bruises morning and evening...

...after I manage to sell the ruined fabrics as if they were choice merchandise, I plan to get totally soused! Get yourself over to Feodosya's this evening. See to it that we get Kuzma the musician—and spread some mustard on his head—and that we have four mademoiselles. Get plump ones.

***

...concerning the IOU—you can take a flying jump! I will gladly proffer a ten-kopeck piece, but concerning the fraudulent bankrupter, we'll see what we shall see.

Finding you in a state of feverish delirium due to the excessive intake of alcohol (delirium tremens), I applied cupping glasses to your body to bring you back to your senses. For these services I request a fee of three rubles.

Egor Frykov, Medical Attendant

Dear Semyon, please don't be angry—I named you as a witness in court concerning that rampage when we were being beaten up, even though you said I shouldn't. Don't act so superior— after all, you yourself caught a couple of wallops too. And see to it that those bruises don't go away, keep them inflamed...

Bill

1 portion of fish soup................1 ruble, 80 kopecks.
1 bottle of Champagne..............8 rubles.
1 broken decanter.....................5 rubles.
Cab for the mademoiselles........2 rubles.
Cabbage soup for the Gypsy....60 kopecks.
Tearing of waiter's jacket..........10 rubles.

...I kiss you countless times, and hope to see you soon at the

———

following address: Fayansov Furnished Rooms, number 18. Ask for Martha Sivyagina.

Your ever-loving Angelica

# AT
# THE
# PHARMACY

I T WAS LATE IN the evening. The
private tutor Egor Alexeyitch
Svoykin, so as not to waste
time, went straight from the doctor's to the pharmacy.

"It's like going from a cowshed into a courtesan's
boudoir!" he thought as he climbed the staircase, which was
polished and covered with an expensive runner. "You're afraid
to put your foot down!"

As he entered, Svoykin was struck by the aroma one finds
in every pharmacy in the world. Science and medicine may
change over the years, but the fragrance of a pharmacy is as
eternal as the atom. Our grandfathers smelled it, and our
grandchildren will smell it too. As it was so late, there were no
customers. Behind a polished yellow counter covered with

labeled jars stood a tall gentleman, his head leaning sturdily back. He had a severe face and well-groomed side-whiskers—to all appearances, the pharmacist. From the small bald patch on his head to his long pink fingernails, everything was painstakingly starched, groomed, licked clean, as if he were standing at the altar. His haughty eyes were looking down at a newspaper lying on the counter. He was reading. A cashier sat to the side behind a wire grille, lazily counting change. On the far side of the counter two dim figures puttered about in the semidarkness, mixing a multitude of strange potions.

Svoykin went up to the counter and gave the starched gentleman the prescription. He took it without looking at it, continued reading the newspaper article to the end of the sentence, and muttered, turning his head slightly: "Calomeli grana duo, sacchari albi grana quinque, numero decem!"

"Ja!" a sharp, metallic voice answered from the depths of the pharmacy.

The pharmacist gave directions for the drops in the same muffled, measured voice.

"Ja!" came from the other corner.

The pharmacist wrote something on the prescription, frowned, and leaning his head back, rested his eyes again on the newspaper.

"It will be ready in an hour," he mumbled through his

---

teeth, his eyes scanning for the sentence he had just finished reading.

"Can't I get it any sooner?" Svoykin muttered. "I can't possibly wait that long."

The pharmacist did not answer. Svoykin sat down on the sofa and waited. The cashier finished counting the change, sighed deeply, and rattled his keys. One of the dark figures in the interior was pounding away with a marble pestle. The other figure shuffled about with a blue vial. Somewhere a clock stuck with rhythmic care.

Svoykin was ill. His mouth was on fire; there was a drawn-out pain in his arms and legs; foggy images tumbled about like clouds and shrouded human figures in his heavy head. He looked as if through a veil at the pharmacist, the shelves of jars, the gas burners, and the cabinets. The monotonous pounding in the marble mortar, and the slow ticking of the clock, seemed to him to be coming not from the outside but from inside his head. The disorientation and fogginess took over his whole body more and more, so that after a while, feeling that the pounding of the pestle was making him sick, he decided to get a hold on himself by striking up a conversation with the pharmacist.

"I think I'm getting a fever," he said. "The doctor says it's a bit soon to tell what I'm suffering from, but I'm already feeling quite weak. Thank God, though, I had the good fortune to fall sick here in the capital and not out in the village, where there's neither doctor nor pharmacy!"

The pharmacist remained stock-still and, leaning his head farther back, kept on reading his newspaper. He didn't respond to Svoykin with word or movement—it was as if he hadn't heard him. The cashier yawned loudly and struck a match against his pants. The pounding of the pestle grew louder and more ringing. Seeing that no one was listening to him, Svoykin lifted his eyes to the shelf of jars and began reading the labels. At first all kinds of herbs shot before his eyes: Pimpinella, Tormentilla, Zedoarian, Gentian, and so on. Behind the herbs, tinctures flashed, -oleums, -seeds, one name stranger and more antediluvian than the next.

"I wonder how much useless ballast there is on these shelves!" Svoykin thought. "How much stuff must be kept in these jars just for tradition's sake, but how solid and impressive it all looks!"

Svoykin moved his eyes from the shelves to the glass cabinet next to him. He saw rubber rings, balls, syringes, jars of toothpaste, Pierrot drops, Adelheim drops, cosmetic soaps, hair-growth ointment.

A boy in a dirty apron entered the pharmacy and asked for ten kopecks worth of ox bile.

"Could you tell me what ox bile is used for?" Svoykin asked the pharmacist, thinking it might be a handy subject for striking up a conversation.

———

Not getting an answer, he stared at the severe and haughty face of the pharmacist.

"God, what strange people they are!" he thought. "Why do they have science stamped all over their faces? Looking at them, you'd think they were lofty scientists, but all they do is sell hair-growth ointment and fleece you. They write in Latin and speak to one another in German... they act as if they're medieval or something. When you're in good health you never notice their dry, stale faces, but the moment you get sick, like me, you're horrified that a sacrosanct profession has fallen into the hands of such rigid, unfeeling characters."

Looking at the pharmacist's motionless face, Svoykin suddenly felt the uncontrollable urge to lie down somewhere in the dark, as far away as possible, away from these scientific faces and the pounding of the marble pestle. The exhaustion of illness took over his whole being. He went up to the counter and, with an imploring grimace, asked:

"Could you please be so kind as to hurry with my medicine! I'm... I'm ill..."

"It'll be ready soon enough... excuse me, but there's no leaning on the counter!"

Svoykin sat down again on the sofa and, chasing away the foggy images in his head, watched the cashier smoke.

"Only half an hour has passed," he thought. "I'm only halfway through... this is unbearable!"

———

But finally the small dark chemist came up to the pharmacist and put down next to him a box with powders and a vial of pink liquid. The pharmacist read to the end of the sentence, slowly walked away from the counter, picked up the vial, and holding it up to his eyes, shook it. Then he put his signature on a label, tied it to the neck of the vial, and then reached for the seal.

"God, what are all these rituals for?" Svoykin thought. "What a waste of time, and they even charge you extra for it!"

The pharmacist turned round and, having finished with the liquid, went through the same procedure with the powder.

"Here you are!" he said finally, without looking up at Svoykin. "Pay the cashier one ruble and six kopecks!"

Svoykin put his hand in his pocket, took out a ruble, and then suddenly remembered that the ruble was all he had.

"One ruble and six kopecks?" he mumbled, embarrassed. "All I have is one ruble... I thought a ruble would be enough... what am I going to do?"

"I have no idea!" the pharmacist said, picking up his newspaper again.

"Under the circumstances... I would be grateful if you would let me bring you, or maybe send you, the six kopecks tomorrow..."

"I'm sorry, we don't give credit here."

"What am I supposed to do?"

"Go home, get the six kopecks, and then you can have your medicine."

"But... I'm having difficulty walking, and I don't have anyone I can send..."

"That's your problem."

"Well," Svoykin thought. "Fine, I'll go home."

He left the pharmacy and set off home. To reach his apartment he had to sit down five or six times. He went inside, found some change on the table, and sat down on his bed to rest. A strange power pulled his head toward the pillow. He lay down for a few minutes. The foggy images, like clouds and shrouded figures, blurred his consciousness. For a long time he kept thinking he had to go back to the pharmacy, and for a long time he intended to get up. But the illness prevailed. The copper coins fell out of his hand, and the sick man dreamed that he had gone back to the pharmacy and was again chatting with the pharmacist.

---

# ON MORTALITY: A CARNIVAL TALE

COURT COUNSELOR Semyon Petrovitch Podtikin sat down at the table, spread a napkin across his chest, and quivering with impatience, awaited the moment the bliny would appear. Before him, as before a general surveying a battlefield, a vista unfolded: rank upon rank of bottles, from the middle of the table right up to the front line—three types of vodka, Kiev brandy, Château La Rose, Rhine wine, and even a big-bellied flask of priestly Benedictine. Crowding around the liquors in artful disarray were platters of sprats, sardines in hot sauce, sour cream, caviar (at three rubles forty kopecks a pound), fresh salmon, and so on. Podtikin greedily ran his eyes over the food. His eyes melted like butter; his face oozed with lust.

---

Frowning, he turned to his wife.

"What's taking so long? Katya!" he called to the cook. "Hurry up!"

Finally, the cook arrived with the bliny. At the risk of scorching his fingers, Semyon Petrovitch snatched up two of the hottest from the top of the pile and slapped them onto his plate with gusto. The bliny were crisp, lacy, and as plump as the shoulders of a merchant's daughter. Podtikin smiled affably, hiccupped with pleasure, and doused the bliny in hot butter. Then, as if to tease his appetite, luxuriating in anticipation, he slowly, deliberately heaped them with caviar. He poured sour cream over the places the caviar left bare. Now he had only to eat, right? Wrong! Contemplating his creation, Podtikin was not quite satisfied. After a moment's thought, he topped the bliny with the oiliest slice of salmon he could find, and a sprat, and a sardine; then, no longer able to hold back, trembling with delight and gasping, he rolled up the two bliny, downed a shot of vodka, wheezed, opened his mouth— and was struck by an apoplectic fit.

---

# A SERIOUS STEP

ALEKSEI BORISITCH HAS just a risen from a deep after-lunch slumber. He is sitting by the window with his wife, Martha Afanasevna, and is grumbling. He is not pleased that his daughter Lidochka has gone for a walk in the garden with young Fyodor Petrovitch.

"I can't stand it," the old man mutters, "when young girls get so carried away that they lose all sense of bashfulness! Loafing about in the garden like this, wandering down dark paths! Depravity and dissipation, that's what it is! You, Mother, are completely blind to it all!... And anyway, as far as you're concerned, it's perfectly fine for the girl to act like a fool... as far as you're concerned, the two of them can go ahead and flirt all they want down there! Why, given half a chance

---

*137*

you too, old as you are, would gladly throw all shame to the winds and rush off for a secret rendezvous of your own!"

"Stop bothering me!" the old woman says angrily. "Look at him, he's rambling on, and doesn't even know what he's rambling about! Bald numskull!"

"Ha! Fine! Have it your way then! Let them kiss and hug all they want! Fine! Let them! I won't be the one called to answer before the Lord Almighty once the girl's head has been turned! Go ahead my children, kiss—court away all you want!"

"Stop gloating! Maybe nothing will come of it!"

"Let us pray that nothing will come of it!" Aleksei Borisitch sighs.

"You have always been your own daughter's worst enemy! Ill will, that's all she's ever had from you! You should pray, Aleksei, that the Lord will not punish you for your cruelty! I fear for you! And we do not have all that long to live!"

"That's all fine and good, but I still can't allow this! He's not a good enough match for her, and besides, what's the rush? With our social status and her looks, she can find herself much better fiancés. And anyway, why am I even talking to you? Ha! That's all I need now, a talk with you! We have to throw him out and lock Lidochka in her room, it's as simple as that! And that's exactly what I'm going to do!"

The old man yawns, and his words stretch like rubber. It is clear that he is only grumbling because he feels a weight in the pit of his stomach, and that he's wagging his tongue just to wag it. But the old woman takes each of his words to heart. She wrings her hands and snaps back at him, clucking like a hen. Tyrant, monster, Mohammedan, effigy, and a string of other special curses fly from her mouth straight at Aleksei Borisitch's ugly mug. The matter would have ended as always with a momentous spit, and tears, but suddenly their eye catches something unusual: Lidochka, their daughter, her hair disheveled, comes rushing up the garden path toward the house. At the same instant, far down in the garden where the path bends, Fyodor Petrovitch's straw hat bobs up from behind the bushes. The young man is strikingly pale. Hesitating, he takes two steps forward, waves, and quickly walks off. Then they hear Lidochka running into the house, rushing through the halls, and noisily locking herself in her room.

The old man and the old woman stare at each other with stunned surprise, cast down their eyes, and turn slightly pale. Both remain silent, not knowing what to say. To them, the meaning behind the fray is as clear as rain. Without a word, both of them understand and feel that while they were busy hissing and growling at each other, their daughter's fate had been decided. The plainest human sensibility, not to mention a parent's heart, can comprehend what minutes of agony Lidochka, locked in her room, was living through, and what an important, fateful role the retreating straw hat played in her life.

Aleksei Borisitch gets up with a grunt and starts marching up and down the room. The old woman follows his every move, waiting with bated breath for him to say something.

"What strange weather we've been having these past few days," the old man suddenly says. "At night it's cold, then during the day the heat's unbearable."

The cook brings in the samovar. Martha Afanasevna warms the cups with hot water and then pours the tea. But no one touches it.

"We should... we should call her... Lidochka... so she can drink her tea..." Aleksei Borisitch mumbles. "Otherwise we'll have to put a fresh samovar on for her... I can't stand disorder!"

Martha Afanasevna wants to say something but cannot. Her lips twitch, her tongue does not obey, and her eyes cloud over. A few moments pass, and she bursts into tears. Aleksei Borisitch, himself teetering on the verge of tears, badly wants to pat the sobbing old woman on the back, but he is too proud. He must stand firm.

"This is all nice and fine," he grumbles. "It's just that he should have spoken to us first... yes... first of all he should have, properly, asked for Lidochka's hand!... After all, we might not want to give it to him!"

———

The old woman waves her hands in the air, moans loudly, and rushes off to her room.

"This is a serious step..." Aleksei Borisitch thinks to himself. "One can't just decide willy-nilly... one has to seriously... from all sides... I'll go question her... find out all the whys and wherefores! I'll talk to her, and then I'll decide... This won't do!"

The old man wraps his dressing gown tightly around himself and slinks to Lidochka's door.

"Lidochka!" he calls, timidly tugging at the doorknob. "Um, are you...um? Are you feeling ill or something?"

No answer. Aleksei Borisitch sighs, shrugs his shoulders for some reason, and walks away from the door.

"This won't do!" he thinks to himself, shuffling in his slippers through the halls. "One has to look at it... from all sides, to chat, discuss... the holy sacrament of marriage, one can't just approach it with frivolity... I'll go and talk to the old woman..."

He shuffles into his wife's room. Martha Afanasevna is standing before an open trunk, rummaging through heaps of linen with trembling hands.

"There's not a single nightshirt here..., " she mumbles. "Good, serious parents will even throw in some baby clothes for the dowry! And us, we're not even doing handkerchiefs and towels... you'd think she wasn't our flesh and blood, but some orphan..."

---

"We have to talk about serious matters, and you're nattering on about bits of cloth... I can't even bear to look at this... our daughter's future is at stake, and she's standing here like some market woman, counting bits of cloth!... This won't do!"

"And what are we supposed to do?"

"We have to think, we have to look at it from all sides... have a serious talk..."

They hear Lidochka unlock her door, tell the maid to take a letter to Fyodor Petrovitch, and then lock the door again.

"She is sending him a definite answer," Aleksei Borisitch whispers. "Ha, the simpleminded fools! They don't have the wherewithal to turn to their elders for advice! So this is what the world has come to!"

"Oh! I suddenly realized, Aleksei!" the old woman gasps, wringing her hands. "We're going to have to look for a new apartment in town! If Lidochka will not be living with us, then what do we need eight rooms for?"

"This is all foolish... balderdash... what we have to do now is to seriously..."

Until dinnertime they scurry about the house like shadows, unable to find a place for themselves. Martha Afanasevna rummages aimlessly through the linen, whispers things to the cook, and suddenly breaks into sobs, while Aleksei Borisitch grumbles, wants to discuss serious matters, and talks nonsense. Lidochka appears at dinnertime. Her face is pink and her eyes slightly swollen.

"So here she is!" the old man says, without looking at her.

They sit down to eat silently for the first two courses. Their faces, their movements, the cook's walk—everything is touched by a kind of shy solemnity.

"We should, Lidochka, you know," the old man begins, "have a serious talk... from all sides... Well, yes!... Um, shall we have some liqueur, huh? Glafira! Bring over the liqueur! Champagne wouldn't be bad either, though, well, if we don't have any... well, forget it... well, yes... this won't do!"

The liqueur arrives. The old man drinks one glass after another.

"Um, so let's discuss things," he says. "This is a serious matter... your future... This won't do!"

"It's simply awful, Daddy, how you just love to talk non-stop!" Lidochka sighs.

"Well, yes," the old man says, startled. "No, you see, I was just... pour se twaddler... don't be angry...."

After dinner, the mother has a long whispered conversation with her daughter.

"I wouldn't be surprised if they're talking pure balderdash!" the old man thinks, pacing through the house. They don't realize, the silly things, that this is serious... important... This won't do! No!"

———

Night falls. Lidochka is lying on her bed awake. The old couple is not sleeping either, whispering to each other till dawn.

"Those damn flies don't let one sleep!" Aleksei Borisitch grumbles. Yet it is not the flies that keep him awake, but happiness.

# THE GOOD GERMAN

I VAN KARLOVITCH SCHWEI, the senior foreman at the Funk & Co. steel mill, had been sent by his boss to the town of Tver to carry out a project. After working on it for some four months, he became so bored without his young wife that he lost his appetite, and on two occasions even burst into tears. During the trip back to Moscow he closed his eyes, imagining how he would arrive home, how Marya the cook would open the door, and how his wife Natasha, with a cry of joy, would throw her arms around his neck.

"She's not expecting me," he thought. "So much the better—unexpected joy is best!"

He arrived in Moscow in the evening. While the porter went to get his luggage, Ivan Karlovitch had time enough to empty two bottles of beer in the station buffet. The beer made him feel very good, and as the cabman drove him from the station to Presnia he kept muttering: "Cabman, you good cabman! I love Russian peoples! You are a Russian man, my wife is a Russian man, and I am a Russian man. My father is German, but I am a Russian man. I wish to secede from Germany!"

Marya the cook opened the door just as he had imagined she would.

"You're a Russian man and I'm a Russian man," he muttered, handing over his luggage to her. "We're all Russian peoples, and we have Russian languages! Where is Natasha?"

"She's asleep."

"In that case, don't wake her... shhh... I'll wake her myself. I want to frighten her, I'll be a surprise! Shhh..."

Sleepy Marya took the luggage and went into the kitchen.

Smiling to himself, blinking, rubbing his hands together, Ivan Karlovitch tiptoed to the bedroom door and opened it carefully, fearing it would creak. It was dark and quiet inside.

"I'm going to startle her," he thought to himself, and lit a match.

But poor German! As the blue sulfur flame of his match flared up, this was the picture he saw: in the bed nearest to the wall, his wife was sleeping, her head covered and only her bare feet showing. In the other bed lay a red-haired giant with long whiskers.

Ivan Karlovitch did not believe his eyes, and lit another

———

match. He lit five matches, one after the other, but the picture remained just as unbelievable, horrifying, and shocking. The German's feet started shaking, and a chill ran down his spine. The beer cloud suddenly lifted, and he felt as if his soul was fluttering up and down his legs. His first thought, his first urge, was to seize a chair and smash it over the sleeping man's red head with all his might, and then grab his unfaithful wife by her bare feet and fling her through the window with such force that she would go crashing down onto the pavement.

"Oh, no! That's not enough!" he decided after some reflection. "First I'll disgrace them! I'll go calling the police and her family, and then I'll be killing them!"

He flung on his coat, and a minute later was out in the street again. He started crying bitterly. He wept and thought of human ingratitude. That barefoot woman had once been a poor seamstress, and he had brought her happiness, turning her into the wife of an educated foreman with a yearly salary of 750 rubles at Funk & Co.! She had been a nobody! She had run around in cotton dresses like some parlor maid, and now, thanks to him, she wore a hat and gloves, and even Funk & Co. called her "Madam."

He thought, "How spiteful and crafty women are!" Natasha acted as if she had married him out of passionate love, and every week she had sent him tender letters in Tver.

"Oh, the snake!" Schwei thought as he walked down the

---

street. "Oh, why did I marry a Russian person? Russian persons are bad! Barbarian, peasant! I wish to secede from Russia, damn me!"

Then he thought, "And what's really surprising is that she exchanged me for some red-haired bastard! If it were Funk & Co. she fell in love with, well, that I could forgive! But to be falling in love with the dog who doesn't have ten kopecks in his pocket! Oh, wretch that I am!"

Schwei dried his eyes and went into a tavern.

"Give me pen and papers," he told the barkeep. "I wish to write!"

With a trembling hand he first wrote a letter to his wife's parents, who lived in Serpukhov. He wrote that a respectable and learned foreman like himself did not wish to live with a tramp of a woman, that they, her parents, were swine, that their daughters were swine, that as far as he was concerned, they could all, they knew what... In conclusion, he demanded that they come and remove their daughter along with the red-headed bastard whom he hadn't killed only because he did not wish to soil his hands!

He left the tavern and dropped the letter in a mailbox. He wandered through the streets until four in the morning, thinking of his sorrow. He looked gaunt and haggard, and came to the conclusion that life, that bitter mockery of fate—that being alive—was foolish and not worthy of a decent German.

————————

He decided not to take revenge on his wife or on the red-headed man. The best thing would be to punish her with a show of great magnanimity.

"I shall go and say to her all I have to say," he thought as he walked home, "and then I'll take my own life! May she be happy with her redheaded man! I shall not stand in their way!"

He imagined how he would die, and how his wife would be tormented by her guilty conscience.

"Yes, I shall leave her my worldly possessions!" he muttered, ringing his doorbell. "The redhead is a better man than I, maybe he earns 750 rubles a year too!"

This time, when Marya the cook opened the door, she was surprised to see him.

"Call Natalia Petrovna," he said, not taking his coat off. "I wish to converse!"

Within minutes his young wife stood in front of him barefoot and in her nightgown, with a startled look on her face. Weeping, throwing his arms in the air, the deceived husband said to her, "I know everything! You can't trick me! With my own eyes I saw the redheaded brute with the long mustache!"

"You're out of your mind!" his wife shouted. "Stop yelling! You'll wake up our boarders!"

"The redheaded bastard!"

"I told you, stop yelling! Look at you, you're drunk out

of your mind and yelling your head off! Go to bed immediately!"

"I have no wish to sleep in the same bed with the redhead! Farewell!

"You've gone completely insane!" his wife shouted furiously. "I told you I've taken in boarders! A locksmith and his wife have moved into what used to be our bedroom!"

"Huh... huh? What locksmith?"

"A red-haired locksmith with his wife! I've rented out the room for four rubles a month! So stop yelling, you'll wake them up!"

The German's eyes bulged as he stared at his wife; then he lowered his head.

"Oh," he whispered.

Soon Ivan Karlovitch's German soul revived again, and he was in a splendid mood.

"For me, you're my little Russian," he muttered. "The cook's a Russian, I'm a Russian, we all have our Russian languages. The locksmith, he's a good locksmith, and I wish to embrace him. Funk & Co. is also a good Funk & Co.! Russia is magnificent land! I wish to secede from Germany!"

# FIRST AID

"MAKE WAY! MAKE WAY! Here comes the sergeant major with his clerk!"

"The compliments of the season, Gerasim Alpatitch!" the crowd shouts. "Let us pray, Gerasim Alpatitch, that the Lord will bless, not you, not us—but whomever he chooses!"

The tipsy sergeant major tries to say something but cannot. He vaguely waves his fingers, goggles his eyes, and forcefully puffs out his fat red cheeks as if he were about to blast the highest note on a trumpet. His clerk, a squat little red-nosed man in a peaked jockey cap, assumes an energetic expression and plunges into the crowd.

"Which of you here is the drowned man?" he asks. "Where's the drowned man?"

"Here! Here!"

The peasants have just pulled a gaunt old man in a blue shirt and bast shoes out of the water. The man is soaked from head to toe and sits on the meadow babbling, his arms spread out and his legs apart. "O saints in heaven! O Christian countrymen of the province of Ryzan and the district of Zaraysk. I've given all I own to my two sons, and now I'm working for Prokor Sergeyev... as a plasterer! Now, as I was saying, he gives me seven rubles and says, 'You, Fedya,' he says, 'you must now worship me like a father!' May a wolf eat him alive!"

"Where are you from?" Egor Makaritch, the clerk, asks him.

"'Like a father!' he says. 'May a wolf eat him alive! And that for seven rubles!'"

"He's babbling! He doesn't even know what language he's talking!" Anisim the squadron leader shouts in a cracked voice, soaked to the waist and obviously upset by the event. "Let me tell you what happened, Egor Makaritch! Come on now, let's have some quiet! I want to explain everything to Egor Makaritch. So the old man's walking over from Kurnevo—come on now, boys, quiet!—Well, so there he is walking over from Kurnevo, and the devil made him cross the river, there where it's shallow. The old man, being a bit tipsy and out of his mind, walked, like an idiot, right into the water, and the current knocked him off his feet and he rolls over like a top! Next thing he starts shouting like crazy. So there I am with Lyksander—what the hell's going on? Why is this man shouting? We look—he's drowning! What are we to do! 'Hey, Lyksander!' I shout, 'Holy Mother of God! Dump that goddamn harmonica and let's go save that peasant!' So we both throw ourselves right into the water, and by God, it's churning and swirling, churning and swirling—O save us, Holy Mother of Heaven! So we get to where it's swirling the most, Lyksander grabs him by the shirt, I by the hair. Then the others here present, who saw what happened, come running up the bank, shouting—all eager to save his soul—what torture, Egor Makaritch! If we hadn't gotten there in time, the old man would have drowned completely, never mind the holiday!"

"What's your name?" the clerk asks the drowned man. "And what is your domicile?"

The old man stares dully into the crowd.

"He's out of his mind!" Anisim says. "And how can you expect him not to be! Here he is, his belly full of water! My dear man, what's your name—no answer! He has hardly any life left in him, only a semblance thereof! But half his soul has already left his body! What a calamity, despite the holiday! What do you want us to do now? He'll die, yes he very well might! His mug is all blue!"

"Hey! You!" the clerk shouts, grabbing the drowned man by the shoulders and shaking him. "You! I'm talking to you! Your domicile, I said! Say something! Is your brain water-logged? Hey!"

———————

153

"Ha, for seven rubles, can you believe that?" the drowned man mumbles. "So I say to him, a dog upon you! We have no wish, thank you very much, no wish...!"

"No wish to do what? Answer clearly!"

The drowned man is silent and begins to shiver with cold, his teeth chattering.

"You can call him alive if you want," says Anisim, "but if you take a good look at him, he doesn't even look like a human being any more! Maybe some drops might help!"

"Drops?" the clerk mimics in disgust. "What do you mean, 'drops'? The man's drowned, and he wants to give him drops! We have to get the water out of him! What are you staring at? You don't have an ounce of compassion, the lot of you! Run over to the village, on the double, and get a rug so we can give him a good shaking!"

A group of men pull themselves away from the crowd and run over to the village to find a rug. The clerk is suddenly filled with inspiration. He rolls up his sleeves, rubs his palms against his sides, and does a series of little movements designed to show his bristling vigor and decisiveness.

"Don't crowd me, don't crowd me!" he mumbles. "All those who are in excess, leave! Did anyone go to the village? Good!"

"Gerasim Alpatitch," he adds, turning to the sergeant major. "Why don't you just go home? You're totally soused, and in your delicate condition it's best to stay home!"

———

The sergeant major vaguely waves his fingers and, wanting to say something, puffs his face up as if it were about to explode in all directions.

"Put him on it!" the clerk barks as the rug arrives. "Grab him by the arms and legs! Yes, that's right. Now put him on it!"

"And I tell him, a dog upon you!" the drowned man mumbles, without resisting or even noticing that he is being lifted onto the rug. "We have no wish to!"

"There, there! Don't worry!" the clerk tells him. "No need to be frightened! We're only going to shake you a bit, and with the help of God you'll come back to your senses. The constable will be over any minute now, and will draw up an official report according to the regulations. Shake him, and praise be the Lord!"

Eight robust men, among them Anisim the squadron leader, grab hold of the corners of the rug. At first they shake him timidly, as if they are not sure of their own strength. But then, bit by bit, they get a taste for it, their faces taking on an intense, bestial expression as they start shaking him with voracious passion. They stretch, stand on tiptoe, and jump up and down as if they want to fly up in the air with the drowned man.

"Heave-ho! Heave-ho! Heave-ho! Heave-ho!"

The squat clerk runs around them, trying with all his might to get hold of the rug, shrieking in a cracked voice:

155

"Harder! Harder! All together now! Keep up the rhythm! Heave-ho! Heave-ho! Anisim! You're lagging! Heave-ho!"

In the split seconds between heaves, the old man's tussled head and pale puzzled face—filled with horror and physical pain—bob up from the rug, but immediately disappear again as the rug flies up to the right, plunges straight down, and then with a snap flies up to the left. The crowd cheers. "Go for it! Save your soul! Yes!"

"Well done, Egor Makaritch! Save your soul! Yes, go for it!"

"Well, boys, and once he's better he'll have to stay right here! Yes, the moment he can stand on his feet, the moment he comes back to his senses, he'll have to buy us all a bucket of vodka for our trouble!"

"Damn! Harnessed poppies on a shaft! Look over there, brothers! It's the lady from Shmelyovo with her bailiff! Yes, it's him. He's wearing a hat!"

A carriage draws up. In it sits a heavy, middle-aged lady wearing a pince-nez and holding a colorful parasol. Sitting next to the driver on the coach box, with his back to her, is Stepan Ivanitch, the bailiff—a young man wearing a straw hat. The lady looks shocked.

"What is going on?" she asks. "What are they doing over there?

"We're reviving a drowned man! Happy holidays, your

---

ladyship! He was a bit tipsy, you see, this is what led to it! We were marching all around the village carrying icons! What a feast!"

"Oh, my God!" the lady gasps. "Reviving a drowned man? But that's impossible! Étienne!" she calls out to Stepan Ivanitch, the bailiff, "for heaven's sake go tell them to stop immediately—they will kill him! Shaking him—this is pure superstition! He must be rubbed and given artificial respiration! Please, go over there immediately!"

Stepan Ivanitch jumps down from the coach box and approaches the shakers. He has a severe look on his face.

"What are you doing!" he shouts at them in a rage. "That's no way to revive a man!"

"So what're we supposed to do?" the clerk asks. "After all, he drowned!"

"So what if he drowned! Individuals unconscious due to drowning are not to be shaken, they are to be rubbed! You'll find it written on every calendar. Put him down immediately!"

Bewildered, the clerk shrugs his shoulders and steps to the side. The shakers put down the rug and look with surprise first at the lady, and then at Stepan Ivanitch. The drowned man, his eyes now closed, is lying on his back, breathing heavily.

"Damn drunkards!" Stepan Ivanitch shouts.

"My dear man!" Anisim says, panting, laying his hand on

his heart. "Stepan Ivanitch! Why such words? Are we pigs? Just tell us plain and simple!"

"You can't shake him, you have to rub him! Undress him! On the double! Grab hold of him and start rubbing! Undress him, on the double!"

"Boys! Start rubbing!"

They undress the drowned man, and under the bailiff's supervision start rubbing him. The lady, not wishing to see the naked peasant, has the coachman drive her a little farther down the road.

"Étienne!" she calls to Stepan Ivanitch. "Étienne! Come here! Do you know how to administer artificial respiration? You must rock him from side to side and press him in the chest and stomach!"

"Rock him from side to side!" Stepan Ivanitch shouts, returning to the crowd. "And press him in the stomach—not so hard, though!"

The clerk, who after his feverish spurt of action is standing around not quite himself, also joins the others in rubbing the drowned man.

"I beg you, do your best, brothers!" he says. "I beg you!"

"Étienne!" the lady calls out. "Come here! Have him sniff burnt leaves and tickle him! Tickle him! Quickly, for God's sake!"

Five minutes pass, ten minutes. The lady looks over at the crowd and notices a commotion. She hears the peasants panting and the bailiff and the clerk barking out orders. A smell of burned leaves and alcohol hangs in the air. Ten more minutes pass, and the peasants keep on working. But finally the crowd parts and the bailiff comes out, red and covered with sweat. Anisim is right behind him.

"He should have been rubbed from the start," says Stepan Ivanitch. "Now it's too late."

"What could we have done, Stepan Ivanitch?" Anisim sighs. "We got to him too late!"

"What is going on?" the lady asks. "Is he alive?"

"No, he died, may the Lord have mercy upon him," Anisim says, making the sign of the cross. "When we pulled him out of the water, there was life in him and his eyes were open, but now he's all stiff."

"What a pity!"

"Well, fate decreed that death would fell him not on dry land but in the water! Could we have a small tip, your ladyship?"

The bailiff jumps onto the coach box, and the driver, glancing over at the crowd as it backs away from the dead body, whips up the horses. The carriage drives on.

———

# INTRIGUES

*a. Election of new chairman of the Association.*
*b. Discussion of the October 2nd incident.*
*c. Synopsis of the activities of member Dr. M. H. von Bronn.*
*d. Routine matters concerning the Association.*

Doctor Shelestov, the culprit in the October 2nd incident, is getting ready to go to the meeting. He has been standing for a long time in front of the mirror, trying to give his face a languid look. If he were to turn up at the meeting with a face that looked concerned, tense, red, or slightly pale, then his enemies would deduce that he was affected by their intrigues. If his face was cold, impassive, as if he had had a good night's sleep, the kind of face that people have who are untouched by the toils and strife of life, then all his enemies would secretly be overcome with respect and think:

———

*His proud rebellious head doth rise higher*
*Than the giddying heights of Napoleon's monument.*

Like a person who has little interest in intrigues and squabbles, he would arrive at the meeting later than all the others. He would enter the room quietly, languidly pass his hand through his hair, and without looking at a single person, take a seat at the very end of the table. Assuming the pose of the bored listener, he would suppress a yawn, pick up a newspaper, and start reading. Everyone would be talking, arguing, boiling over, calling each other to order—but he would remain silent, reading his newspaper. Then finally, as his name was repeated more and more often and the burning question turned white-hot, he would lift his bored, weary eyes and say to his colleagues, reluctantly:

"You are forcing me to speak... Gentlemen, I have not prepared a speech, so please bear with me—my words cannot do this scandal justice. I shall begin ab ovo. At the last meeting some of our esteemed colleagues asserted that I do not conduct myself in an appropriate manner during medical consultations, and consequently they called me to account. Being of the opinion that I need not proffer justifications, and that the accusations are nothing but unscrupulous ploys, I asked that my name be removed from the membership roster of the Association, and subsequently resigned. Now, however, that a whole series of new accusations are being leveled against me, I find, to my great regret, that I am forced to offer an explanation after all. With your permission, I shall explain."

At this point, carelessly twirling a pencil or a chain, he would say that yes, in actual fact it was true that during consultations he had sometimes been known to raise his voice and attack colleagues, regardless of who was present. It was also true that once, during a consultation, in the presence of doctors and family members, he had asked the patient, "Who was the idiot who prescribed opium for you?" Rare was a consultation without incident... But why was this? The answer was simple! In these consultations he, Shelestov, was always saddled with colleagues whose knowledge left much to be desired. There were thirty-two doctors in town, most of whom knew less than a first-year medical student. One didn't have to look far for examples. Needless to say, nomina sunt odiosa—one does not wish to name names—but as they were among themselves at the meeting, and he did not want to appear a scandalmonger, names would be mentioned. For instance, everyone was aware that our esteemed colleague von Bronn pierced the esophagus of Madam Seryozhkina, the official's wife, when he inserted a probe.

At that point von Bronn would jump up, wring his hands, and cry out: "My dear colleague, you were the one who stabbed her, not I! I'll prove it!"

---

Shelestov would ignore him, and continue: "Furthermore, as everyone is aware, our esteemed colleague Zhila mistook the actress Semiramidina's floating kidney for an abscess and undertook a probing puncture. The immediate result was exitus letalis—lethal consequences! Our esteemed friend Besstrunko, instead of removing the nail from the big toe of a left foot, removed the healthy nail from the right foot. I am also pressed to recall the case in which our esteemed colleague Terkhayantz catheterized the soldier Ivanov's eustachian tubes with such vigor that both his eardrums exploded. I would also like to remind you that this very same colleague of ours, while extracting a tooth, dislocated the patient's lower jaw and wouldn't reset it until the patient agreed to pay him five rubles for the procedure. Our esteemed colleague Kuritsin, who is married to the pharmacist Grummer's niece, is running a racket with him. Everyone is also aware that the secretary of our Association, your young friend Skoropalitelni, is living with the wife of our highly valued and esteemed chairman, Gustav Gustavovitch Prechtel... You will notice that I have delicately moved from discussing lack of medical knowledge to unethical behavior. I have no choice! Ethics is our weak point, gentlemen, and so as not to appear a mere scandalmonger, I will call to your attention our esteemed colleague Puzirkov, who at Colonel Treshinskoy's name-day party told everyone that it was not Skoropalitelni

---

who was living with our chairman's wife, but I! The effrontery of Mr. Puzirkov, whom I myself caught last year with the wife of our esteemed colleague, Dr. Znobish! Speaking of Znobish—who is it that uses his position as a doctor and can't quite be trusted when treating ladies? Znobish! Who is it that married a merchant's daughter for her dowry? Znobish! And as for our highly esteemed chairman, he secretly dabbles in homeopathy and receives money from the Prussians for espionage! A Prussian spy—that is the ultima ratio!"

When doctors wish to appear clever and eloquent they use two Latin expressions: nomina sunt odiosa and ultima ratio. Shelestov would drop not only Latin words but French and German ones as well—whatever you want. He would steer everyone to clear waters, rip the masks off the intriguers' faces. The chairman would ring his bell till he was exhausted—esteemed colleagues would be flying up from their seats all over the place, yelling and waving their arms—colleagues of every denomination would fall over each other in a heap:

Zip-bang-wham-bang-wham-bang-wham!

Not batting an eyelash, Shelestov would continue: "And as for this Association, its current membership and organization being what it is, it is inevitably headed for destruction. Its whole structure is based exclusively on intrigues. Intrigues, intrigues, intrigues! I, as one of the victims of a mass of demonic intrigues, consider myself bound to expound the following...."

He would go on expounding, and his supporters would applaud and clasp their hands together in exultation. At this point, with an unimaginable uproar and peals of thunder, the voting for the new chairman would commence. Von Bronn and his cohorts would heatedly support Prechtel, but the public and the ethical group of doctors would boo them and shout, "Down with Prechtel! We want Shelestov! Shelestov!"

Shelestov would consent, but on condition that Prechtel and von Bronn ask his forgiveness for the October 2nd incident. Again there would be an unimaginable clamor, and again the esteemed colleagues of the Jewish faith would fall over each other in a heap: "Zip-bang-wham!" Prechtel and von Bronn, seething with indignation, would end up resigning from the Association. Not that he would care!

Shelestov would end up as chairman. First he would clean out the Augean stables. Znobish—out! Terkhayantz—out! The esteemed colleagues of the Jewish denomination—out! With his supporters he would see to it that by January not a single intriguer would be left in the Association. The first thing he would do would be to have the walls of the Association's clinic painted, and hang up a sign saying "Absolutely No Smoking." Then he would fire the medical attendant and his wife, and medicine would henceforth be ordered not from the Grumer pharmacy but from the Khryashchambzhitskov pharmacy. All doctors would be forbidden to perform operations without his supervision, etc. And most important, he would have visiting cards printed, saying "Chairman of the Association of Doctors."

Thus Shelestov dreams as he stands at home in front of his mirror. But the clock strikes seven, reminding him that it is time to leave for the meeting. He shakes himself awake from his sweet thoughts and hurriedly tries to give his face a languid expression, but—alas! He tries to make his face languid and interesting, but it does not obey, and instead becomes sour and dull, like the face of a shivering mongrel puppy. He tries to make his face look firm, but it resists and expresses bewilderment, and it seems to him now that he does not look like a puppy but like a goose. He lowers his eyelids, narrows his eyes, puffs up his cheeks, knits his brow, but all to no avail... damn!... he cannot get the right expression. Obviously, the innate characteristics of that face are such that you couldn't do much with them. His forehead is narrow; his small eyes flit about nervously, like those of a cunning marketwoman; his lower jaw juts out somehow absurdly and stupidly; and his cheeks and hair give the impression that this "esteemed colleague" has just been kicked out of a billiard parlor.

Shelestov looks at his face, flies into a rage, and begins sensing that his face is plotting against him. He goes out into the hall, and as he is putting on his coat, his galoshes, and his hat, he feels that they are intriguing against him too.

———

"Cabbie, to the clinic!"

He hands the cabbie twenty kopecks, and the intriguing cabbie asks for twenty-five. He sits in the droshky going down the street; the cold wind beats him in the face, the wet snow flies into his eyes, the horse drags its feet. Everything is conspiring to intrigue against him. Intrigues, intrigues, intrigues!

---

# PART TWO

*In his twenties Chekhov wrote many humorous sketches, skewed aphorisms, vignettes, and comical glossaries. These appeared in the early 1880s in magazines such as* Strekoza *(Dragonfly),* Budilnik *(Alarm Clock), and* Oskolki *(Splinters), under headings such as "This and That," "Trifles," and "Gnats and Flies." Chekhov's work in this genre has been neglected for many years, but today it is coming into its own as important experimental work that anticipated the absurdist movement by over forty years.*

# THIS AND THAT:

# FOUR VIGNETTES

I T IS A BEAUTIFUL FROSTY DAY. Sunbeams play on every drop of snow. There is no wind, no cloud.

A couple is sitting on a bench on the boulevard.

"I love you," he whispers.

Little pink cupids flush over her cheeks.

"I love you," he continues. "When I first set eyes upon you, I understood why I am alive—I saw the aim of my life! It is either life with you—or absolute nonexistence! Marya Ivanovna! My dearest! Yes or no? Marya! Marya Ivanovna... I love... my darling Marya... Please answer me, or I shall die! Yes or no?"

She raises her eyes and looks at him. She wants to say yes; she opens her mouth.

"Yuck!" she screams. On his snow-white collar, racing past each other, are two gigantic bugs... how disgusting!!

"Dearest Mama," an artist wrote to his mother, "I'll be coming to visit you! Thursday morning I'll have the pleasure of pressing you to my heart that is so full of love for you! To heighten the pleasure of our seeing each other again, I shall bring... Go on, guess! No, Mama, you'll never guess! I'll bring with me that marvel of beauty, that pearl of human art! I shall bring (I can see you smile) the Belvedere Apollo!"

"My darling Nicolai," his mother wrote back. "I am so happy that you are going to visit me. May the Lord bless you! But come on your own; don't bring Mr. Belvedere! There's hardly enough to eat for the two of us."

The air is full of soothing fragrances: lilacs, roses. A nightingale sings, the sun is shining... and so on.

Under a spreading acacia tree on a bench in the town park sits a high school senior in his new uniform. He wears a pincenez on his nose, and a little mustache. Beside him sits a pretty young thing.

The student is holding her hand. He trembles, turns pale, blushes, and whispers words of love.

"Oh, I love you! If you only knew how much I love you!"

"And I love you!" she whispers back.

The student puts his arm around her waist.

"Oh life! How blessed you are! I am drowning, I'm trans-

---

ported with happiness! Plato was right when he said... Oh, just one kiss! Olya! Just one kiss!"

Languidly she lowers her eyes. How she thirsts for this kiss! His lips stretch toward her pink lips. The nightingale sings even louder.

"Get back to your class!" a resonant tenor voice booms above the student's head.

The student lifts his head, and his cap falls off. The school inspector is standing in front of them.

"Get back to your class!"

"But it's our lunch break, sir!"

"You have a Latin class! You will have to stay two hours after school today!"

The student stands up, puts on his cap, and leaves. As he leaves, he feels her eyes resting on his back. Behind them, the inspector's footsteps.

They are playing Hamlet:

"The fair Ophelia!" Hamlet shouts. "Nymph, in thy orisons be all my sins remembered!"

"The right side of your beard has come off!" Ophelia whispers.

"Be all my sins remembered!... huh?"

"The right side of your beard has come off!"

"Damn!! To a nunnery, go!"

---

173

# ELEMENTS MOST OFTEN FOUND IN NOVELS, SHORT STORIES, ETC.

COUNT, A COUNTESS still showing traces of a once great beauty, a neighboring baron, a liberal man of letters, an impoverished nobleman, a foreign musician, slow-witted manservants, nurses, governesses, a German bailiff, a squire, and an heir from America. Plain faces, but kind and winning. The hero—whisking the heroine off a bolting horse—courageous and capable in any given situation of demonstrating the power of his fists.

Heavenly summits, immense, impenetrable distances... in a word, incomprehensible nature!

Fair-haired friends and red-haired foes.

A rich uncle, open-minded or conservative, depending on

*175*

circumstances. His death would be better for our hero than his constant demands.

An aunt in the town of Tambov.

A doctor with an anxious face, giving hope in a crisis; often he will have a bald pate and a walking stick with a knob. And where there's a doctor, there is always rheumatism that arises from the difficulties of righteousness; migraine; inflammation of the brain; nursing of wounds after duels; and the inevitable prescribing of water cures.

A butler, in service for generations, ready to follow his master into the fire. A superb wit.

A dog so clever he can practically speak, a parrot, and a thrush.

A dacha outside Moscow and an impounded estate in the south.

Frequent purposeless references to electricity.

A wallet made of Russian leather; Chinese porcelain; an English saddle. A revolver that doesn't misfire, a medal on a lapel, pineapples, champagne, truffles, and oysters.

Inadvertently overheard words that suddenly make everything clear.

An immeasurable number of interjections and attempts at weaving in the latest technical terms.

Gentle hints at portentous circumstances.

More often than not, no ending.

———

Seven deadly sins at the beginning and a wedding at the end.

The end.

—————

# QUESTIONS POSED BY A MAD MATHEMATICIAN

1. I was chased by 30 dogs, 7 of which were white, 8 gray, and the rest black. Which of my legs was bitten, the right or the left?

2. Ptolemy was born in the year 223 a.d. and died after reaching the age of eighty-four. Half his life he spent traveling, and a third, having fun. What is the price of a pound of nails, and was Ptolemy married?

3. On New Year's Eve, 200 people were thrown out of the Bolshoi Theater's costume ball for brawling. If the brawlers numbered 200, then what was the number of guests who were drunk, slightly drunk, swearing, and those trying but not managing to brawl?

4. What is the sum of the following numbers?

5. Twenty chests of tea were purchased. Each chest contained 5 poods of tea, each pood comprising 40 pounds. Two of the horses transporting the tea collapsed on the way, one of the carters fell ill, and 18 pounds of tea were spilled. One pound contains 96 zolotniks of tea. What is the difference between pickle brine and bewilderment?

6. There are 137,856,738 words in the English language, and 0.7 more in the French language. The English and the French came together and united their two languages. What is the cost of the third parrot, and how much time was necessary to subjugate these nations?

7. Wednesday, June 17, 1881, a train had to leave station A at 3 a.m. in order to reach station B at 11 p.m.; just as the train was about to depart, however, an order came that the train had to reach station B by 7 p.m. Who is capable of loving longer, a man or a woman?

8. My mother-in-law is 75, and my wife 42. What time is it?

# AMERICA IN ROSTOV ON THE DON

THE FOLLOWING CURIOUS notice adorned the last couple of issues of the *Don Bee*:

My wife, Efrosinya Alexandrovna, ran away—"to find some love and happiness"—with an army officer. As I am perfectly happy without her, I ask, first of all, that she never come back again, and second, that whoever might find her does not deliver her back here, and third, that I refuse to recognize any further extensions to my lineage, except for our two children, Alexander (4), and Yevgeni (4 months).

*Yakov Selvestovich Ribalkin*

This notice led us to the following modest reflections:

---

1.   What if somebody does find this treacherous woman and, ignoring the notice, brings her back to the esteemed Mr. Ribalkin? What then?

2.   How much will the esteemed Mr. Ribalkin be paid per line? This "tale from his life" is so interesting that the Don Bee's readership has increased at least threefold in the last few days. Although it would not surprise us if the honorarium for this piece went to Mr. Ter-Abramian, himself—"the Pumblisher [!] and Enditor [!]" This editor is obviously under the misapprehension that the above piece is a bona fide announcement. He refuses to acknowledge that there might well be other humorists beside himself.

3.   The style of this announcement reminds one too much of Mr. Ter-Abramian's own style. Could this be a joke at the expense of the public on the part of the great publisher himself?

# MR. GULEVITCH, WRITER, AND THE DROWNED MAN

O N FRIDAY, JUNE 10, the famous and talented journalist Ivan Ivanovitch Ivanov took his own life in the Hermitage gardens, in front of everyone. He drowned himself in the pond. May you rest in peace, you honest and noble toiler, whisked away in the prime of life. (The deceased was not yet thirty.)

That same Friday, in the morning, the deceased had taken some pickle brine for his hangover, written a playful sketch, lunched cheerfully with friends, gone for a walk in the park with some cocottes at seven in the evening, and at eight... taken his life!

Ivan Ivanovitch was known to be joyful, carefree—a lover of life.

---

He never thought of death, and had not once boasted that he would live "God knows how long," even though he drank like a fish. So you can imagine the expressions on the faces of all who knew him when his body was pulled out of the green water!

Rumors raced through the park—"There's something fishy going on! This smells of foul play! The deceased had no creditors, no wife, no mother-in-law... he loved life! There is no way he would have drowned himself!"

The suspicion of foul play grew stronger when the ventriloquist, Mr. Egorov, attested that a quarter of an hour before Ivanov's tragic end, he had seen the deceased in a boat with Mr. Gulevitch, writer. When the authorities undertook a search for Mr. Gulevitch, it turned out that the writer had made a run for it.

Arrested in Serpukhov, Mr. Gulevitch, writer, at first claimed he knew nothing. Then, when he was told that a confession would mitigate his guilt, he burst into tears and confessed. At the preliminary inquest he made the following deposition:

"I knew Ivanov only for a short time. I became acquainted with him because I have a great respect for men of the press. [In the protocol the word respect was underlined.] There were no family ties between us, nor did we have any business connections. On the ill-fated evening, I had invited him for tea

---

and stout, because I have great respect for literature [here again respect was underlined, and next to it in scrawny protocol handwriting, 'All this emphasis!']. After tea, Ivan Ivanovitch said, 'Wouldn't it be nice to take a boat out.' I agreed, and we got into a boat.

"'So tell me a joke!' Ivan Ivanovitch said when we were in the middle of the pond.

"I didn't need to be asked twice, and launched into one of my classical jokes with 'Well, if you insist.' After only a few words Ivan Ivanovitch burst out laughing, grabbing his stomach, rocking back and forth, causing the deciduous [What does he mean?] foliage of the Hermitage gardens to resound with the congenial [What?] hilarity of the venerable journalist... When I, Gulevitch, writer, finished my second joke, Ivan Ivanovitch again burst out laughing, rolled back... It was Homeric laughter! Only a Homer [Who?] could laugh thus! He rolled back, leaned against the side... the boat listed, and the silvery ripples obfuscated him from Mother Russia's loving eyes... and... I can't go on! Tears... are choking me!"

This deposition did not quite match the deposition given by Mr. Egorov. The venerable ventriloquist stated that Ivanov was by no means laughing. Quite the contrary. While he was listening to Mr. Gulevitch, writer, his face was sour and doleful in the extreme. Mr. Egorov had been on the shore, and had heard and seen how at the end of the second anecdote Ivanov had clasped his head and exclaimed: "How stale and boring life is! What melancholy!"

It was after he uttered these words that he tumbled into the water.

The law will now have to decide which of the two depositions is more credible. Mr. Gulevitch has been released on bail.

The death of Mr. Ivanov was not the first fatal incident in the Hermitage Park, and it is high time someone took measures to protect the public from future incidents of this nature... By the way, I'm only joking.

_____

# THE POTATO AND THE TENOR

HOW DANGEROUS FOODS can sometimes be is seen in the following excerpt from the medical journal the *Physician's Whistle:*

The other day I was convinced yet again of the danger of starchy foods (writes Dr. B.). The tenor Mr. Sh——mov visited me at the polyclinic, complaining of tightness and cramping of the throat. When I inspected his throat with a mirror, I noted that a potato the size of an egg was lodged against his vocal cords. The potato was already bloated and had begun to sprout. I asked the poor tenor how this had happened, and he explained that the potato had become embedded in his throat five years before, and had already borne fruit five times.

187

"In five years I have coughed up five sacks of potatoes!" he said with a bitter smile.

When I suggested that the patient undergo surgery, he refused point-blank, insisting that the potato in no way impeded his singing. I asked him to sing something. He was kind enough to oblige, and sang an aria from Cagliostro. Indeed, he could still sing.

"But isn't it a problem that your voice resembles the howl of a young jackal?" I asked him.

"No, not at all," the tenor answered.

The *Physician's Whistle,* no. 22

———

# MAYONNAISE

ASTRONOMERS REJOICED when they discovered spots on the face of the sun. A case of unparalleled malice!

An official took a bribe. At the very moment of the fall, his boss entered and looked suspiciously at his clenched fist, in which the illicit bank note lay. The official was deeply embarrassed.

"Excuse me!" he called after the petitioner, holding out his palm. "You forgot something in my hand!"

When is a goat a pig?

"Somebody's goat had started coming over to our goats," a landowner told us. "We caught the goat and gave it a good hiding. But it still kept coming over. So we gave it a real thrashing and tied a stick to its tail. But that didn't help either. It still managed to get at our goats. Fine! We caught it, spread tobacco on its nose, and smeared it with turpentine. After that it didn't show up for three days, but then there it was again! Now isn't that goat a pig?"

Exemplary resourcefulness:

When the Saint Petersburg reporter N.Z. visited the textile exhibition last year, he noticed one pavilion in particular and began writing something down.

"I think you just dropped a twenty-five ruble note," the exhibitor in the pavilion said, handing him the note.

"I dropped two twenty-fivers!" the reporter shot back.

The exhibitor was so amazed at this resourcefulness that he gave him a second twenty-fiver.

This really happened.

---

# AT A PATIENT'S BEDSIDE

**D**OCTORS POPOV AND MILLER *are standing by a patient's bed, arguing.*

POPOV: I must confess that I'm not a strong believer in conservative methods.

MILLER: My dear colleague, I haven't said a word about conservatism... it's up to you what you believe or don't believe, what you acknowledge and what you don't acknowledge. What I'm saying is we need, in concreto, a change in regime.

THE PATIENT: Oh! *(With difficulty he rises from the bed, walks to the door, and peeks apprehensively into the next room.)* Nowadays even the walls have ears!

POPOV: The patient is complaining about oppression—tightness in the chest—the feeling of not being allowed to breathe. We'll have to resort to strong measures.

*The patient groans and looks fearfully toward the window.*

MILLER: But before we go to extremes, I suggest we scrutinize his constitution.

THE PATIENT *(turning pale)*: Gentlemen, please don't speak so loud! I'm a civil servant, a family man! People are walking by right outside the window.... I have servants! Oh! *(He wrings his hands despairingly.)*

———

# MY
# LOVE

SHE, AS MY PARENTS and my bosses authoritatively affirm, had been born before me. Whether this is true or not, all I know is that I don't remember a single day in my life when I didn't belong to her, when I didn't feel under her power. She doesn't leave my side night or day, and I myself would never think of walking out on her— our bond, you might say, is powerful, lasting. But do not be jealous, young girls reading these words! This touching bond brings me nothing but misery! First of all, in not leaving my side night or day, she will not let me do the things I need to do. She won't let me read, write, go for walks, enjoy nature. Now, as I write these lines, she pulls me by the elbow and, like Cleopatra of ancient times, tries to drag me, her Antony, toward the bed. Secondly, she ruins me like a French courtesan. For her affections I have sacrificed everything: career, glory, and comfort. Because of her I go about dressed in rags, live in poor lodgings, eat meager scraps of food, write in pale ink. She consumes everything, everything—she is insatiable! I detest her, despise her! I should have sought a divorce long ago, but until now I haven't done so—and not because Moscow lawyers charge four thousand for a divorce, either. We don't have children so far. Oh, you would like to know her name? With pleasure. It is a name that begins with an L, as in Lily, Lizzy, Lalya.

Her name is: LAZINESS.

# A GLOSSARY OF TERMS FOR YOUNG LADIES

I F A DILIGENT SCHOOLGIRL loves studying physics, then this is physical love.

When young people declare love in a car, it's carnal love.

If a young lady doesn't love you, but your brother, then it's brotherly love.

When people love spraying themselves with scents, then this is sensual love.

When an elderly maid loves dogs, cats, and animals in general, then this is an animalistic love.

---

Husband is the word for a man who, out of pity and by police injunction, helps fathers feed and clothe their daughters.

A rutting life is postmen and coachmen trotting in autumn down broken, rutted roads.

# DATES OF FIRST PUBLICATION IN PERIODICALS

"Sarah Bernhardt Comes to Town" (I to, i syo: Pis'ma i telegramy Antoshi Ch.), Zritel, no. 23–24., December 6, 1881.

"On the Train" (V vagone), Zritel, no. 9, 1881, signed "Antosha Ch."

"The Trial" (Sud) Zritel, no. 14, 1881, signed "Antosha Chekhonte."

"Confession; or, Olya, Zhenya, Zoya: A Letter" (Ispoved' ili Olya, Zhenya, Zoya: Pis'mo) Budilnik, no. 12, 1882.

"Village Doctors" (Sel'skiye eskulapy), Svet i teni, July 18, 1882, no. 22, signed "Antosha."

"An Unsuccessful Visit" (Neudachny vizit), Oskolki, November 27, 1882, no. 48, signed "A man without a spleen."

"A Hypnotic Seance" (Na magneticheskom seanse), Zritel, January 24, 1883, no. 7, signed "A man without a spleen."

"The Cross" (Krest) Oskolki, February 12, 1883, no. 7, signed "A man without a spleen."

"The Cat" (Kot), Oskolki, May 14, 1883, no. 20, signed "A. Chekhonte."
"How I Came to Be Lawfully Wed" (O tom, kak ya v zakonny brak vstupil: Rasskazets), Oskolki, no. 24, June 11, 1883, signed "A. Chekhonte."

"From the Diary of an Assistant Bookkeeper" (Iz dnevnika pomoshchnika bukhgaltera), Oskolki, no. 25, June 18, 1883.

"A Fool; or, The Retired Sea Captain: A Scene from an Unwritten Vaudeville Play" (Dura, ili kapitan v ostavke: Stsenka iz nesushchestvuyushevo vodevilya), Oskolki, September 17, 1883, no. 38, signed "A. Chekhonte."

"In Autumn" (Osenyu), Budilnik, no. 37, 1883.

"The Grateful German" (Priznatel'ny nemets), Oskolki, no. 46, October 1, 1883, signed "A man without a spleen."

"A Sign of the Times" (Znameniye vremeni), Oskolki, no. 43, October 22, 1883, signed "A man without spleen."

"From the Diary of a Young Girl" (Iz dnevnika odnoy devitsy), Oskolki, no. 43, October 22, 1883, signed "A man without spleen."

"The Stationmaster" (Nachal'nik stantsii), Oskolki, no. 45, November 5, 1883, signed "A. Chekhonte."

"A Woman's Revenge" [Mest' zhenshchiny], Russkii Satiricheskii Listok, no. 2, February 2, 1884, signed "Anche."

"O Women, Women!" (O zhenshchiny, zhenshchiny!), Novosti Dnya, February 15, 1884, no. 45, signed "Anche."

"Two Letters" (Dva pis'ma), Oskolki, March 10, 1884, no. 10, signed "A man without a spleen."

"To Speak or Be Silent" (Govorit' ili molchat': Skazka). Written in late March or early April of 1884. First published in Krasnii Arkhiv, 1925.

"After the Fair" (Yarmochnoye "itovo"), Razvlechenie, no. 36, September 13, 1884.

---

"At the Pharmacy" (V apteke), Peterburgskaya Gazeta, July 6, 1885, no. 182, signed "A. Chekhonte."

"On Mortality: A Carnival Tale" (O brennosti: Maslyanichnaya tema), Oskolki, no. 8, February 22, 1886, signed "A man without a spleen."

"A Serious Step" (Seryozny shag), Oskolki, no. 26, June 28, 1886, signed "A. Chekhonte."

"The Good German" (Dobry nemets), Oskolki, no. 4, January 24, 1887, signed "A. Chekhonte."

"First Aid" (Skoraya pomoshch), Peterburgskaya Gazeta, no. 168, June 22, signed "A. Chekhonte."

"Intrigues" (Intrigi), Oskolki, no. 43, 1887.

"This and That: Four Vignettes" (I to, i syo. Poeziya i proza), Zritel, no. 16, 1881, signed "Antosha Ch."

"Elements Most Often Found In Novels, Short Stories, Etc." (Chto chashche vsevo vstrechayetsya v romanakh, povestyakh, i t.p.), Strekoza, no. 26, July 29, 1880, signed "Antosha."

"Questions Posed by a Mad Mathematician" (Zadachi sumasshedshevo matematika), Budilnik, no. 8, 1882, signed "Antosha Chekhonte"

"America in Rostov on the Don" (Amerika v Rostove-na-Donu), Zritel, no. 21, March 21, 1883, signed "A man without a spleen."

"Mr. Gulevitch, Writer, and the Drowned Man" (Koe Chto), Budilnik, no. 23, 1883, signed "My brother's brother."

"The Potato and the Tenor" (Koe Chto), Budilnik, no. 23, 1883, signed "My brother's brother."

"Mayonnaise" (Mayonez) Oskolki, September 17, 1883, no. 38, signed "A man without a spleen."

---

"At A Patient's Bedside" (U posteli bol'novo), Oskolki, no. 48, December 1, 1884, signed "A man without a spleen."

"My Love" (Moya ona), Budilnik, no. 22, 1885, signed "My brother's brother."

"A Glossary of Terms for Young Ladies" (Slovotolkovatel' dlya "baryshen'"), Oskolki, no. 28, July 12, 1886, signed "A man without a spleen."